WOLF
BLOOD

Pull of the Moon

ROBERT
RIGBY

Piccadilly
PRESS

To Megan

First published in Great Britain in 2015 by
PICCADILLY PRESS
80–81 Wimpole St, London W1G 9RE
www.piccadillypress.co.uk

Based on the series created by Debbie Moon

This is a work of fiction. Names, places, events and incidents are either the products of the author's imagination or used fictitiously. Any resemblance to actual persons, living or dead, is purely coincidental.

A CIP catalogue record for this book is available from the British Library.

ISBN: 978-1-84812-517-9
also available as an ebook

1

Typeset by Palimpsest Book Production Ltd, Falkirk, Stirlingshire

Printed and bound by Clays Ltd, St Ives Plc

Piccadilly Press supports the Forest Stewardship Council (FSC), the leading international forest certification organisation, and is committed to printing only on Greenpeace-approved FSC-certified paper.

Piccadilly Press is an imprint of Bonnier Publishing Fiction, a Bonnier Publishing company
www.bonnierpublishingfiction.co.uk
www.bonnierpublishing.co.uk

Prologue

The full moon hung like a bloated silver ball in the night sky, casting a ghostly light on the farmhouse and the desolate moorland.

Nothing moved, nothing stirred, but from a downstairs window the flicker of a television screen sent jagged shadows dancing on the stone walls of the outhouse buildings.

Inside the house, in the comforting warmth of the living room, Maddy Smith lay back on the sofa and gazed at the TV, seeing but not reading the movie credits as they rose slowly and almost hypnotically up the screen.

It was late; Maddy had enjoyed the film almost as much as she had enjoyed the accompanying giant-sized bag of popcorn and large bar of chocolate. She was not usually up this late on a school night, but there had been no one around tonight to order her up to bed. Maddy was alone, and making the most of it. But her eyelids were beginning to droop, and now that the bag of popcorn was completely empty, the film was over and even the credits had stopped rolling, she decided it was finally time to turn in.

She raised the remote to switch off the DVD player and then froze.

A sound; outside. It was faint, yet Maddy heard it quite clearly. She pressed a button on the remote and the television screen went dark.

More sounds. A thud and then a door slamming, shattering the stillness of the night.

Maddy was instantly wide awake; senses wired. She got up from the sofa and padded across the room, her bare feet noiseless on the cold stone floor.

Reaching the hallway, she glanced down and saw her school shoes close to the front door. She stepped into them, almost without pausing, not stopping to tie the laces, and then opened the door.

The wind had risen, wispy strands of cloud scudded across the face of the moon, but the light remained vivid. A metallic crash came from somewhere at the back of the house and a shadow of fear crossed Maddy's face. But she stepped out from the front doorway into the cold night and moved quickly towards the source of the sound.

She paused at the far end of the side wall and peered around to the back. The stark moonlight highlighted an overturned dustbin and scattered rubbish. Maddy tensed, fear mounting, but she knew there was no alternative; she had to confront the terror.

And then she saw it. A wolf, huge and grey, razor-sharp teeth glinting in the moonlight as it ripped apart the carcass of a chicken scavenged from the upturned dustbin.

Sensing Maddy's presence, the wolf whipped its head around, and golden eyes glinted a vicious warning, fixing the trembling teenager with a withering stare.

Maddy stood momentarily paralysed with fear; her worst nightmare had come true.

Behind the wolf, the wooden shutters to the coal chute dropping into the cellar lay wide open, the metal latch smashed away by the sheer power of the wolf's ferocious assault.

And as Maddy took in the full scene, she saw a second wolf, smaller and brown, leaping up from the depths of the cellar, battling to join its companion.

The grey wolf had not moved; its eyes remained fixed on Maddy's. Threatening, daring her to move closer.

'Get back inside!' she yelled, stepping nearer.

The grey wolf hesitated, seeming surprised at the response to its threat. But then it sprang forward, moving like lightning, trying to dart past the girl barring its way.

Maddy was just as fast, dodging one way and then the other as the wolf made its bid for freedom. She took one step closer and then another, forcing the wolf to move backwards, back towards the gaping coal chute.

The wolf growled its frustration, crouching low as though preparing to spring into the attack.

Maddy's eyes widened, not in fear this time, but in defiance. And as she too sank to the ground and went on to all fours, her own eyes turned a liquid golden yellow and she bared her teeth.

And then Maddy growled, just as menacingly and threateningly as the grey wolf had done.

It was a battle of wills that Maddy dared not lose. She growled again, and as the grey wolf took a faltering step back over the chute it suddenly lost its footing and plunged into the cellar. At the same time, the brown wolf was making its leap for freedom.

Moving even faster, Maddy whipped off one of her shoes and smacked the wolf on the nose. As it dropped back with a yelp, a lunging paw knocked the shoe from Maddy's hand and it too plummeted downwards.

Without stopping to think, Maddy slammed the shutters closed and shoved an iron bar between the handles. Now there was no escape.

Maddy stood up, breathing hard, and a long sad howl came from the depths of the cellar and echoed away towards the moors.

One

Maddy had slept late; it was hardly surprising. She hurried down the stairs dressed in her school clothes, but shoeless. Pausing momentarily at a second staircase leading to the cellar door, she thought back to the previous evening. With a sigh and a shake of her head she continued on down to the cellar.

The darkness was illuminated by a single light bulb. Maddy took a bunch of keys from a nail in the brick-work. Three locks clicked open one after another and then Maddy pulled back the heavy door.

Her mum and dad, Emma and Daniel, stood waiting in their den, beneath the moon-like glow of a light hanging from the low ceiling. Both parents looked more than a little guilty as they smiled a sheepish good morning to their daughter.

Daniel rubbed his stomach. 'I think that chicken was off.'

Maddy had no sympathy. 'I can't believe you! Breaking out and raiding the bins!'

She was about to continue with her tirade when she spotted her shoe on the floor. Chewed and still wet with saliva, it was totally ruined. 'Oh, Mam!'

Emma sighed and shrugged her shoulders, as if to say, Well, what do you expect?

'You're always saying we have to stay hidden from humans, never give in to our wolf-self, but the moment you get the chance you try to break out,' Maddy protested.

'You don't understand how powerful the pull of the moon is,' her dad said, leading the way up from the den and into the kitchen.

Emma drew back the curtains and blinked at the bright morning light. She turned to Maddy. 'When you're old enough to take wolf form –'

'I won't be a hypocrite who says stay hidden and then breaks out at the first whiff of food,' Maddy said, interrupting. She glared at her dad. 'And that chicken! Yuck!'

Daniel quickly changed the subject. 'You were still dressed when you came outside.'

'And you know the rule,' Emma added, 'bed by ten on school nights.'

It was Maddy's turn for a hasty change of subject. 'I'll miss the bus. I have to go.'

She hurried out to the hallway to grab her coat.

Her mum was determined to have the last word. 'And don't you ever hit me on the nose again!'

* * *

Bradlington High School sat high in the Northumbrian countryside, at one end of a wide valley, with panoramic views of woodlands, moorlands and distant hills.

Maddy was fourteen and in Year 9. And she was enduring an embarrassing start to the new school week, having turned up in wellington boots. They were the first footwear that had come to hand when she'd rushed from the house, but she regretted her impulsive choice the moment she clomped on to the school bus and heard the laughter.

It got worse when she arrived at school. First she had to run the gauntlet of Jimi Chen, Sam Dodds and Liam Hunter, who as usual took great delight in finding a victim to tease. Then she came face to face with three more classmates, namely Kara, Katrina and Kay – famously know throughout the school as the Three Ks. The Ks were always together and dedicated followers of fashion, from their identical earrings to their stylish shoes. So the sight of Maddy in wellington boots made them reel away in horror.

And when Maddy met up with one of her two best mates it didn't get better. Tom Okanawe was a great friend: caring, kind, fiercely loyal and a good laugh, but even Tom couldn't resist a comment when he spotted the wellies. 'What *have* you got on your feet!'

There was no way Maddy could explain what had actually happened so she tried to be funny. 'My shoes got eaten by werewolves. Didn't you see the full moon?'

But the attempt at humour didn't work. Tom raised his eyes to the heavens. 'Oh, don't you start,' he said. 'I've already heard enough of werewolves and beasts from –'

'Maddy!' a voice boomed from across the playground.

Maddy turned to see her other best friend, Shannon Kelly, hurtling towards them. Shannon was not only the brainbox of the class, she also had an unshakeable belief that something beastly was lurking on Stoneybridge Moor. And she was constantly on the hunt for evidence to back up that belief.

'– Shannon,' Tom added, as their friend came bustling up, brandishing her phone.

'Did you hear it?' Shannon said excitedly to Maddy. 'On the moor, howling?'

'Hear what?' Maddy said, thinking she would much rather Shannon teased her about the wellington boots than delve too deeply into sounds coming from the moor.

But Shannon didn't even notice the boots. 'And look,' she said, holding up her phone, 'I took this photo on Drayman's Lane this morning. It's evidence.'

Maddy stared at the photo in disbelief. It was a close-up of something looking exactly like a wolf's paw print. But that was impossible; her dad had got no further than the yard and her mum had not even made it out of the cellar.

'I'm going to compare this to paw prints of different dogs,' Shannon said excitedly.

'What, every type of dog?' Tom asked.

'Yes, if I have to. This is proof, Tom; proof that there's something weird out there on the moors.'

By the time Maddy, Shannon and Tom reached their lockers and Maddy had swapped the wellington boots for her gym shoes, Shannon was more determined than ever to hunt down the mysterious beast.

She was detailing her plans when their form teacher, Mr Jeffries, came marching down the corridor, stopping to speak to them. 'Ah, just the people I want to see.'

'Yes, sir?' Maddy said brightly, glad of the interruption.

'This photography club of yours,' Mr Jeffries said, 'it's got to go!'

'What?' the friends said in unison.

'But you can't close us down, sir,' Maddy added quickly. 'The camera club is a vital part of school life.'

'With three members,' Mr Jeffries said. 'You three!'

'But we're getting more,' Shannon said, pointing at a nearby noticeboard. 'Look at our *members wanted* notice, sir. I can see new signatures.'

Mr Jeffries peered at the notice. 'Oh, yes, the Incredible Hulk wants to join, and Superman and Batman too.'

'Who did that?' Maddy said angrily, tearing the notice from the board.

'I'm not really interested,' Mr Jeffries continued. 'Look, it's good that you three enjoy photography, but that doesn't entitle you to a room on school premises to use as your own private den.'

'It's our darkroom,' Tom said.

'Darkroom, den, doesn't matter. You have until tomorrow morning to find at least three new members or I'm closing you down.'

'But . . .'

It was too late. Mr Jeffries was already striding down the corridor, leaving Maddy, Shannon and Tom to follow gloomily towards morning registration.

But Maddy suddenly stopped. Her Wolfblood senses had engaged. Wolfblood senses brought the world into a heightened, much sharper focus. Maddy could see more, hear more, smell more. There was something wrong. Something different. Something out of place.

She stood perfectly still, inhaled slowly and immediately picked up a scent that was familiar. She had to track the scent to its source; it was so strong she could almost see it. Leaving Tom and Shannon, she moved back towards the playground, the scent growing stronger all the time.

She knew she was nearing her target when the bell for registration sounded and a stampede of kids came rushing through the doors. The scent was instantly weakened and confused, and by the time the crowd cleared it had gone completely.

Maddy sighed, a puzzled frown on her face.

The classroom was buzzing; there was plenty to talk about after a weekend. Jimi and his mates were in their usual seats near the back, the Three Ks were deep in fashion discussion, while at the front of the room, Mr Jeffries stood speaking to a new arrival. 'And I'm head of year as well as your form tutor, so you'll see a lot of me.' He turned to the rest of the class. 'Everyone, this is Rhydian Morris, who, I'm guessing, is from Wales?'

'No,' the new boy said bluntly.

'Ah, right,' Mr Jeffries said, amid laughter from around the classroom. 'OK, he's not from Wales.'

All eyes were on Rhydian. Jimi and his friends stared challengingly while the Three Ks looked on with serious interest. Tall and fair, Rhydian was certainly good-looking, though his face was sullen and hostile. But to the Three Ks, that made him even more interesting.

All the attention was on Rhydian, so Maddy was fortunate that her late arrival sparked no one's attention. But the moment she stepped into the room she was again aware of the familiar scent. It was even closer now and almost overpowering.

She raised her eyes and stared at the new boy and saw that he was staring back at her – equally surprised and equally confused.

'What are you *doing* here?' Maddy hissed.

Rhydian was sitting alone in the dining hall at lunchtime. He was drawing, sketching in a pad, but he covered up his work at the sound of Maddy's voice.

'What?'

'Here! On our territory! Don't you know the rules?'

'What are you on about?'

'Look, you can't stay here!'

Rhydian was about to get to his feet to continue the argument when Tom ambled up and glimpsed the partially revealed drawing. It was a dark and mysterious forest in a snow blizzard.

'Hey, that's brilliant,' Tom said.

Rhydian's eyes were still fixed on Maddy's, but he moved his arm to reveal the rest of the drawing. Leaping from the swirling snow was a wolf, fangs bared, eyes wild with bloodlust.

'Wow,' Tom said, 'that is seriously scary.'

'What do you want?' Rhydian said to Tom but looking at Maddy.

'I just wondered if you like football?'

'Not much.'

'It's a good way to make friends. When you're somewhere new, I mean.'

Rhydian turned his head and glared at Tom. 'Look, I don't like football, and I don't want to hang out with you . . .' he glanced momentarily at Maddy, '. . . or your weirdo mate. You got that?'

'Yeah, I've got that.' Tom was a nice guy, but he was no pushover. He gestured to Maddy. 'Come on, Maddy. Obviously they don't teach manners in Wales.'

'And I'm not from Wales!' Rhydian called as they walked away.

Neither Maddy nor Tom looked back, but after they'd found a table on the far side of the room they noticed the Three Ks walk up to Rhydian and sit, uninvited, at his table.

Maddy watched, engaging her wolf hearing so that she could hear every word that was said.

'Look at this,' Kay said to Rhydian, brandishing a magazine. 'It's a competition, Teenage Model of the Year.'

'We're going to enter,' Katrina added.

'And we think you should, too,' Kay said. 'You're dead good-looking.'

The two girls giggled while across the room Maddy shook her head and groaned.

Katrina was trying her best to grab Rhydian's undivided attention. 'All you need is a . . . what's it called . . . a photolio?'

Kay rolled her own eyes. 'She means a portfolio.'

Kara, the natural leader and generally the smartest of the Three Ks, decided it was her turn to make her play for the new boy. 'He's not interested in the competition, girls, he's only just got here.' She leaned closer to Rhydian. 'What he needs is someone to show him around.'

Across the room, Maddy could not stop herself from laughing. It was the slightest of chuckles but Rhydian heard it. As Maddy looked over at him again she saw his eyes locked on to hers.

And then she heard him speak quietly to Kara. 'That weird girl, who is she?'

Kara glanced briefly at Maddy before turning back to Rhydian. 'Oh, that's Maddy Smith. She's from one of those country families; lived here for centuries. They never leave the area and they don't like strangers.' She leaned even closer. 'Now me, I'm much more interesting.'

Two

The future, or possible non-future, of the photography club was weighing heavily on Tom and Shannon as lunch break drew to a close. Maddy had other things on her mind, but as always she was trying to be supportive of her friends.

They had retreated to the darkroom, which was crammed with old photographic equipment as well as a small stock of cheap digital cameras and a computer. There was also a tattered armchair and a couple more rickety chairs. In truth, Mr Jeffries was right; it was a den as much as a clubroom, and Maddy and the others didn't want to lose it.

'To attract new members, we need a better image,' Tom said. 'And a catchy name, something cool, like . . . Snap Attack!'

Maddy shook her head. 'That is terrible.'

'How about . . . Snaptastic?'

Maddy didn't even bother replying to that one.

'I've got it!' Shannon said excitedly. 'Miss Parish's badger stakeout!'

Tom frowned. 'That is definitely not a catchy name.'

'No! It's happening, Miss Parish's badger watch. Today, I think. There's a sign-up list on the board by the lockers.'

'And how will that help us get three new members?'

'It's open to anyone. If we go and we dish out all the club cameras, I'll bet we get at least three new members by the time it's over.'

Maddy nodded. 'It's the best idea yet.'

As they approached the lockers, Maddy spotted Rhydian again. He was opening the door to his own, newly allocated locker. Jimi and his friends, Sam and Liam, lurked nearby. They were grinning and their grins turned to laughter as Rhydian pulled open the door to discover a leek propped inside.

'Is that your lunch, Welshie?' Jimi laughed.

'I'm not Welsh!' Rhydian snarled, grabbing the vegetable.

Jimi turned away, still laughing, and his friends followed. But the laughter stopped as the leek thudded into Jimi's back. It didn't hurt, but that wasn't the point. He swung around, glaring at Rhydian, and then strode back to him.

They stood eyeball to eyeball for a moment and then Jimi raised both hands and shoved Rhydian so that he fell against the lockers.

There was a blur of movement as Rhydian leapt high into the air and smashed into Jimi, sending him tumbling. Before Jimi could react Rhydian was on him, eyes wild, teeth bared in a snarl. Jimi whimpered in shock and terror.

The veins in Rhydian's arms were starting to flow with a dark, silver liquid. Maddy had seen the warning signs and as Rhydian got to his feet, she grabbed him by the arm and dragged him away. 'Come on!'

A crowd was gathering, most eyes focused on the dazed Jimi, so Maddy hurriedly pulled Rhydian back to the darkroom, pushed him inside and locked the door.

But he was losing control. 'What are you doing?' he yelled.

'It's all right, Rhydian, just breathe.'

'No! Get out!'

'Breathe, slowly.'

'You have to get out! You have to!'

It was too late; Rhydian could no longer control his actions. He jack-knifed away, crashing into shelves, sending boxes and files flying. When he looked towards Maddy again she could see cloudy silver liquid surging up the veins in his neck.

'I'm so sorry,' Rhydian groaned. 'So . . .'

Canine teeth were forming in his mouth; his eyes were turning gold. He dropped to the floor and swiftly, almost instantly, the transformation was complete, and Maddy was staring at an almost fully grown wolf.

Panic-stricken, wolf-Rhydian raised his head and spun around in circles, searching for a way out. But there was no escape. The wolf leapt on to the table, sending photographic equipment and developing chemicals crashing.

'Rhydian!' Maddy shouted.

The yell made wolf-Rhydian jump to the floor, crouch low and focus golden eyes on Maddy, with fangs bared. A vicious snarl emerged from his throat.

Somehow, Maddy stayed calm. She took a backwards step and then slowly dropped into a similar crouched position. She bowed her head and remained that way for several long moments. When she raised her head her eyes, too, were gold.

Wolf-Rhydian stared and their eyes met. And then he too bowed his head; a sign of recognition and mutual acceptance had passed between them.

Maddy let out a long shivering breath and was suddenly aware of the commotion out in the corridor. She got to her feet and went to listen at the door.

Jimi was complaining loudly to Mr Jeffries. 'He attacked me, sir! He's off his head.'

'And where is Rhydian?'

'I don't know. He must have run off.'

'I'll catch up with him later. In the meantime, you come with me.'

Maddy sighed with relief and turned around. The

wolf had gone. Rhydian was back in his human form but pale, shaking and sweating as he stared at Maddy. 'I knew there was something about you when I first saw you. Then in here, when your eyes went . . . It's true, isn't it? You're like me!'

Maddy was furious. 'I'm not like you! I don't show off and pick fights and invade other packs' territory. You're a danger to us all and the sooner you leave the better!'

Three

Bernie's was more than a café and a shop; it was the unofficial social centre of Stoneybridge. The owner, unsurprisingly called Bernie, sold everything from crisps to plastic rain macs, and was usually the first to know anything worth knowing. He was gruff and gossipy, but good-hearted too.

He was watching Shannon now as she tried to decide on which chocolate bar to choose. Maddy and Tom stood waiting; they were about to join Miss Parish and her badger watchers, who were gathering outside.

'Are you going to buy something or not?' Bernie said to Shannon.

Shannon finally took a chocolate bar from the rack and was handing over the money as the Three Ks walked in.

Tom smiled. 'Don't tell me you three are coming on the badger watch?'

Kay rolled her eyes. 'As if.'

'Hey, Bernie,' Kara said, 'has Rhydian come in?'

'Who?'

'Well, he's tall, and dreamy.'

'And Welsh.' Katrina added.

'He is not Welsh, Katrina!' Kara said.

'Oh,' Bernie said, 'you mean the Vaughans' new foster kid.'

Maddy was suddenly interested. 'Rhydian's in foster care?'

'Oh, aye. Must have been a bad boy to get moved all the way up here for a fresh start, eh?'

Maddy quickly handed the cameras she was carrying to Tom. 'You and Shannon can give these out. I'll meet you in the woods.'

'But –'

But Maddy was gone. Outside the shop she sniffed the air and then smiled – she had picked up Rhydian's scent.

Rhydian had been running, hurtling through the woods. Fast. Faster than anyone who'd seen him would have thought possible. Now he was walking along a lane, heading towards his foster parents' place and deep in thought.

He was confused. He'd always wanted to meet another kid like him but now that it had finally happened, he'd been totally rejected. He was hurt and angry and ready to move on. Clear out.

He heard footsteps approaching from behind. 'Rhydian?'

He spun around. 'Don't worry,' he snapped, as Maddy came closer. 'I'm out of here.'

'I'm sorry, I was stupid,' Maddy said. 'Look, I know about the Vaughans. I know you're alone. Listen, we can help you.'

'Help? I've had help. Counselling, Ritalin. It didn't help.'

'But we can *really* help. You need to learn to control your wolf-self before someone gets hurt, probably you.' Maddy paused. 'I'm like you, you saw that.'

Rhydian shook his head. 'You may be like me, but you think like everyone else. You want to make me better, but you don't see that what I am, what I turn into, that *is* better. It's the best feeling ever, and no one's taking it away from me.'

He went to walk on but Maddy grabbed his arm. 'I'm not letting you go.'

Rhydian gave an instinctive snarl and yanked himself free. 'Stop me. Go on; try. Then see how long it takes for someone to find out what you are. Because none of your mates know your little secret, do they?'

Maddy didn't reply and Rhydian smiled. 'Thought not. See, I've got nothing to lose here. Unlike you.'

And with that he turned and ran, with incredible speed, leaping over a gate into a field and headed for the woods. Maddy's eyes widened. She could never match that speed. But then something instinctive told her that she could. She had to do it.

So she did.

She cleared the gate as easily as Rhydian had and found herself hurtling into the woods hot on Rhydian's heels. Then they were running together, weaving through the woodland, dodging trees at breakneck speed, ducking under branches without pausing, splashing though shallow streams, leaping a huge rock, faster and faster.

They neared a dip into the valley, and then Maddy playfully jumped at Rhydian, catching him on the legs, and they both went tumbling, rolling downwards over a cushion of fallen leaves and twigs.

They sat up, breathless, grinning at each other, just as Miss Parish and twenty or more students, including Tom and Shannon, stood up from their badger observation spot behind a huge fallen tree trunk.

Maddy and Rhydian exchanged a look.

'Er . . . sorry, we're late,' Maddy said, blushing furiously. 'Seen any badgers yet?'

'No!' Miss Parish bellowed. 'And you two have scared off every animal for miles!' She turned to the other pupils. 'I'm sorry, everyone, but the badger watch is over! Ruined!'

She stomped away and the badger watchers followed,

dumping cameras into the hands of Tom and Shannon as they went.

Shannon made one last effort. 'So, who's signing up for photography club, then?' No one replied and Shannon turned to Maddy. 'Oh, well done, Mads!'

'Sorry,' Maddy said, 'but there was something I had to do.'

'And it was more important than the photography club?'

'Well, yes, actually, Rhydian is more important than the club!'

Tom and Shannon stared and even Rhydian's eyes widened at Maddy's words. She could hardly believe she had said them herself.

'You see . . .' Maddy didn't quite know how to continue.

'Yes?' Shannon said.

'You see . . .'

'Yes?' Tom said.

'Well . . . Rhydian and me are related!'

No one said a word, so Maddy went on, 'We're distant cousins; he's the black sheep of the family. And I didn't want him here so I treated him badly, which is why he sort of lashed out.'

'And trashed our darkroom,' Shannon said, glaring accusingly at Rhydian, who said nothing.

'But the thing is,' Maddy continued, 'he's part of my life now, and that's that.'

Tom and Shannon looked at each other for a few long moments. Then Tom shrugged his shoulders and smiled.

Shannon nodded. 'OK,' she said to Maddy. 'Sure.'

The four of them walked back to Stoneybridge in a slightly embarrassed silence. As they approached Bernie's the Three K's came hurrying out to meet them.

'We have a proposition for you,' Kara said to Maddy.

'Oh yes?'

'This modelling competition, it'll cost us too much to get our photos done professionally.'

'So?'

'So, if you take our photos, we'll join your photography club.'

'You?'

'Oh, don't worry, we're not going anywhere near your manky darkroom. We'll just put our names down so Jeffries keeps it open. Deal?'

Maddy glanced at Maddy and Tom and they both nodded.

'Deal.'

'So if you're not from Wales, how did you get called Rhydian?' Maddy asked Rhydian as she walked part of the way home with him that evening.

'My mum was Welsh. I think.'

'And how long have you been in care?'

'Since I was two.'

'And nobody knows who you are?'

Rhydian was reluctant to give too much away. 'I don't know a lot; my mum abandoned me, that's all.'

'So what did you do for the full moon last night?'

This time Rhydian grinned. 'Couldn't stay in my room, could I? I climbed out through the window.'

'So it was *your* paw print Shannon found.'

'And what about you? Full moons must be epic out here.'

Maddy looked embarrassed. 'I . . . I haven't started transforming yet.'

'Oh,' Rhydian said, smiling, 'so I know more about this stuff than you do?'

'Oh, yeah, you're the expert. That's why you lost it with Jimi in front of half the school.'

'I didn't know it could happen,' objected Rhydian. 'Last night was only my second change.'

'Yeah, well, we feel the urge to change when we're threatened or angry, too. Learn to control it and you can transform whenever you want.'

'I thought werewolves only went hairy at full moon,' Rhydian said. 'How do you know all this stuff?'

'My parents tell me.'

'You've got parents like us?'

'Yes. And it's Wolfblood, not werewolf. We're not monsters.'

'But the weird thing is,' Rhydian said, 'I don't even remember being bitten.'

Maddy laughed. 'Bitten! You weren't bitten! We're *born* as Wolfbloods; part wolf and part human. We're different from most people, that's all, but there's nothing wrong with that. We can still fit in and lead a normal life.' She smiled. 'And make friends.'

They walked on, Rhydian lost in thought for a while. 'I'm not making any promises,' he said eventually, 'but say I do stay around? For a while?'

'Then you'll have a pack at last; people to teach you.'

'Oh, no. No rules and no lectures. You can keep your group hugs and your big furry family. I do things my way.'

'Oh, I see. A lone wolf, eh?'

Rhydian nodded slowly. 'That's right, a lone wolf.'

Four

The following morning Emma Smith was happy to drive her daughter to school. She wanted to catch a glimpse of the newly arrived Wolfblood. And there was more.

'Don't forget to invite him round for dinner tomorrow night,' she said to Maddy as the Land Rover drew to a standstill outside the school. 'We need to talk to him about transforming safely.'

'I doubt he'll come, Mam,' Maddy said, reaching for the door handle. 'He's a loner. Let me talk to him first.'

'No, Maddy, invite him round.' Emma glanced out at the thronging mass of kids making their way into school. 'Which one is he, anyway?'

She didn't need Maddy to answer. Her eyes widening, she sniffed the air for the trace of a scent and quickly located Rhydian as he slouched towards the entrance doors. 'That's him, isn't it?'

Maddy nodded and pushed open the car door. 'Can't hide anything from a Wolfblood.'

'Poor lad, imagine going through all this on your own.'

'I have to go, Mam.'

Emma smiled. 'Tell him Wednesday's hog roast night.'

Maddy hurried into school but stopped and stared in horror as she entered the corridor leading to her registration classroom. Every window in the long corridor was plastered with an identical poster featuring a photograph with a short caption scrawled underneath:

THE MOORS MONSTER –
PROOF AT LAST!

Maddy pulled one of the posters from the glass. It showed a grainy woodland scene with a fallen tree in the foreground. The shot had been zoomed in several times so had lost its sharpness but beneath the tree, in the shadows, was . . . something; a strange shape, the suggestion of glaring eyes and bared teeth.

'Oh, Rhydian,' Maddy breathed. 'You idiot!'

She hurried to the classroom to see Shannon waiting by the door and surrounded by excited classmates. Even the Three Ks were impressed. 'It's so scary,' Katrina said, 'where did you get it?'

'Took it myself this morning,' Shannon answered proudly. 'I made the posters in the darkroom.'

'It's amazing,' Kara said.

'Yeah,' Kay added. She smiled. 'Seriously, Shannon, we always thought you were just a bit mental.'

'Thanks,' Shannon said, grinning; nothing could deflate her joy this morning.

Tom was proud of his friend. 'It is evidence,' he said, peering closely at the photograph. 'It looks like a wolf.'

Maddy remained silent. She needed to speak urgently to Rhydian, who was across the corridor staring at another copy of the poster. He looked worried, as worried as Maddy felt, but before she could push her way through the crowd he hurried away.

Jimi Chen and his mates Sam Dodds and Liam Hunter came sauntering up. Jimi enjoyed being the centre of attention and was always keen to mock Shannon's efforts to hunt down the beast of the moors. He also had a copy of the poster. 'You call this proof?' he said loudly.

'Yes, I call it proof,' Shannon replied firmly. 'What do you call it?'

Jimi grinned. 'Photoshop.'

There was a burst of laughter followed by the nodding of heads. It seemed that some of those entirely convinced by the photo just moments earlier were ready to change their minds and agree with Jimi.

'Laugh all you like,' Shannon said confidently, 'but I've got the camera in the darkroom with the original files on the memory card – you can't fake those!'

'Fine,' Jimi smirked. 'Let's see them, then.'

* * *

The darkroom had never been so crowded. Everyone wanted to see the original photographs Shannon claimed to have taken that morning. But, just as Maddy suspected, when they searched for the memory card it could not be found.

Shannon was devastated. 'It was here!' she said, glaring at the grinning Jimi. 'Someone took it!'

'Oh, yeah, we know,' Jimi mocked. 'It's a conspiracy, everyone's against you.'

'Leave it, Shannon,' Maddy said to her friend, knowing the situation could only get worse.

'No!' Shannon shouted, her eyes fixed on Jimi. 'You took it, didn't you, to make me look an idiot.'

'You don't need my help with that,' Jimi laughed, walking off with his grinning friends.

The remaining onlookers also drifted away, until only Shannon's two staunch friends, Tom and Maddy, remained.

'He took it,' Shannon said, close to tears. 'I know he did.'

Maddy knew differently. Rhydian had been here, very recently. His scent still lingered in the darkroom.

First lesson was art. It was Rhydian's favourite subject but he had no chance to settle down to his work as Maddy was quickly at his side. 'You took that memory card,' she said in little more than a whisper.

'Yeah,' Rhydian murmured, 'you can thank me later.'

'You made Shannon look stupid.'

'Tough.'

Maddy was struggling to keep her voice down. 'If you hadn't been wolfing about in the woods she wouldn't have got a picture in the first place.'

'It wasn't me!'

'What?' Maddy realised she was speaking too loudly. She lowered her voice. 'Then who was it? Our pack hasn't been sighted for years, then suddenly you come along and Shannon has a picture.'

'Oh, and it couldn't have been your parents?'

'They don't wolf out in public! You took that card to protect yourself.'

'I took it to protect us!' Rhydian snapped. He reached into his shirt pocket and threw the memory card on to the desk. 'But if you'd rather protect your friend's reputation, then go ahead.'

He stared down at the blank sheet of drawing paper in front of him; the conversation was over.

It was a difficult, tense day. Maddy kept the memory card with her, trying to decide what to do with it. She and Rhydian avoided each other while Shannon spent every free moment in the darkroom and Tom kept any thoughts he had about the mysterious photograph to himself.

But by the end of the day it looked as though interest in the photo was fading, much to Maddy's relief. Then she spotted a new poster made by Shannon. It had a photograph of a memory card with the caption –

HAVE YOU SEEN THIS MEMORY CARD?
CONTACT SHANNON KELLY!

Maddy was about to go looking for Shannon when she came storming by, brushing past without stopping to speak.

Maddy hurried after her. 'Are you OK?'

'Oh, fine,' Shannon said, still not stopping. 'Apart from the fact that I'm a laughing stock, *and* I just got a lunchtime detention for tomorrow.'

'Why?'

This time Shannon did stop. 'Apparently photocopying thirty posters is a misuse of school property. Plus I got a warning for fighting.'

'You what!'

'I was frisking Liam; he shoved me so I cracked him one!'

'Shan!'

'I need to find that card, Maddy!'

'Come on, Shan,' Maddy said gently, trying to placate her friend. 'Come round to mine? We'll nick Dad's chocolate biscuits and watch some films.'

Shannon sighed and shook her head. The rage was gone. 'No,' she said sadly, 'think I'll just go home.'

Rhydian unfolded a crumpled copy of Shannon's original poster and compared the photograph to the scene before his eyes. He was in the right place. The large fallen tree trunk was unmistakeable and the shadowy spot where something had lurked was clearly visible.

But *what* had lurked in the shadows? Rhydian sniffed the air and then studied the ground, looking for tracks, but there were no clues in the woodland leaf litter. Crouching down by the tree trunk, he spotted scratches in the bark. Claw marks.

Nothing but the occasional burst of birdsong disturbed the silence. And then Rhydian heard a different sound. A sniff. He rose slowly to his feet, his Wolfblood senses engaging. Another sniff told him that someone, or something, was on the far side of the trunk.

He edged forward, moving cautiously but ready to spring into action. He craned his neck, looked around the trunk, and saw Shannon. She was sitting on the ground, her camera at her side. And she was crying.

Rhydian started to creep away, not wanting to embarrass Shannon, but a twig snapped underfoot. She looked up and saw him. Hurriedly wiping her eyes, she stuffed the camera into her bag.

'Looking for that monster again, eh?' Rhydian said, trying to sound cheerful.

'Leave it, Rhydian,' Shannon snapped.

'Nope,' Rhydian said simply. He went to the tree and sat next to Shannon. 'So why are you so interested in it, then?'

Shannon stared at him, thinking for a moment that he too was going to make fun of her. But his gentle smile encouraged her to answer. 'I saw something, years ago. I was seven, on a camping trip with the Brownies, not far from here. I shared a tent with Kay.'

'Kay!' Rhydian said, surprised. 'As in the Three Ks, Kay?'

Shannon nodded. 'She was my best friend then. I couldn't sleep; there were sounds outside. I was playing shadow monsters on the side of the tent with my torch. Then . . .' she paused for a moment, remembering, '. . . then there was a real shadow, outside. I turned off my torch; I thought it was one of the others. So I unzipped the tent to look and there it was.'

'What?'

'This . . . this face. Hairy, with yellow eyes. I screamed; woke the whole camp. By the time they got to me the monster had disappeared. But I freaked out Kay and the others so much they called off the rest of the trip.'

'So . . . so what do you think it was?'

Shannon shrugged. 'I don't know. When I got back to school every one had heard, then they started making fun of me. I was even sent to a child psychologist.'

'What for?'

'I wouldn't shut up about it. Everyone said I did it for attention.'

Rhydian nodded. This was beginning to sound familiar. 'It's not nice to be accused of lying, is it?'

Shannon nodded. 'Exactly.'

Five

'I think today is veggie day.'

Rhydian turned to see Maddy standing behind him in the lunch queue. 'What? Really?'

'Wednesday usually is.'

'Oh no,' Rhydian groaned.

It was the first time they had spoken since their row in the art room the previous day.

'I'm sorry about the memory card,' Maddy said. 'You were right to take it.'

'Yeah. Totally.'

The memory card appeared to be the last thing on Rhydian's mind; he was thinking about food. So it seemed the right moment for Maddy to mention the invitation. 'Will you come to dinner tonight? Mam and Dad want to talk about . . .' she lowered her voice, '. . . wolfing out, safely. I know its embarrassing but if we could just get it out of the way?'

'Out of the way,' Rhydian said, showing no interest at all. 'Yeah. Right.'

'Rhydian! You're not listening to me!'

'Eh? What? Are you certain it's veggie day?'

'Yes! But what's . . .?' Maddy stopped, and then she smiled. 'Oh, I get it. Meat. You've got cravings.'

'Cravings!' Rhydian looked desperate. 'They're vegetarians, Maddy. My foster parents; vegetarians.'

Maddy laughed. 'Well, Wednesday's hog roast night out our place.'

Rhydian's eyes widened. 'Hog roast?'

'You know, a whole pig roasted. And all the trimmings.'

'Trimmings?'

'Mmmm. Bacon, sausages. Fancy it?'

'Oh yes,' Rhydian breathed. 'Yes. But right now I can't face another vegetable.'

He hurried away while Maddy waited in the queue and chose a perfectly tasty macaroni cheese knowing that she too could look forward to the hog roast that evening.

After lunch Maddy and Tom headed off for the darkroom, where they suspected Shannon might be lurking. But it wasn't Shannon who'd been busy with photographic work.

Jimi Chen had pasted a picture of Shannon's head on to her own photograph of the supposed beast of the moors. And he'd kept the caption, which read –

THE MOORS MONSTER – PROOF AT LAST!

As Jimi showed the poster around, everyone thought it hilarious – everyone but Shannon. She'd got her first glimpse just as Maddy and Tom walked up, and one look was enough. With a snarl of fury, Shannon hurled herself at Jimi.

'Oh, the monster's attacking me,' Jimi screamed in mock terror. 'Help me, please, somebody help me!'

Maddy and Tom ran forward and tried to drag Shannon away.

'What on earth is going on here?' Mr Jeffries shouted, rushing up.

The laughter stopped but Jimi was quickest to respond. He pointed at Shannon. 'She attacked me, sir! She needs help!'

Mr Jeffries spotted the new version of the poster. 'When is all this going to stop?' he said to Shannon.

'The monster's real, sir,' Shannon answered. 'And I'll prove it.'

'Then you'll have to do it after detention.'

'What? Another one?'

Mr Jeffries' eyes fell on Maddy, Tom and Jimi. 'All four of you, right now. Follow me.'

'That's what we get for trying to help,' Tom whispered to Maddy as they trailed dejectedly behind their form teacher.

The detention seemed to drag on and on. Mr Jeffries was at his desk, working through a pile of marking, Maddy and Shannon sat together doing some homework and Tom was at the next table, doing nothing. Jimi sat behind them, staring at the ceiling.

'I meant what I said,' Shannon said to Maddy, speaking more loudly than was wise. 'We'll find that monster tonight.'

'But I can't tonight. I've got this dinner thing with my parents.'

'Then get out of it.'

'I can't, it's important to them.'

Shannon sighed loudly. 'Fine.' She glanced across at Tom. 'Tom's coming, aren't you, Tom?'

Tom didn't look enthusiastic. 'Well, there's this Man U match on tonight . . .'

He stopped when he saw Shannon's icy glare.

'. . . which I will record.'

'Good,' Shannon said. 'Meet at Bernie's, five o'clock.'

Two desks behind them, Jimi was grinning. And plotting.

Rhydian was desperate for the taste of meat. The table was almost groaning under the weight of roast pork, ham, bacon and sausages and Rhydian was working his way speedily through as much of it as he could manage.

He had exchanged self-conscious greetings with Maddy's parents on his arrival but had barely said another word since sitting at the table. He was too busy eating.

Maddy cringed as she watched him pick up a pork-chop bone and suck noisily on it, devouring every last trace of meat. Her parents were highly amused.

'Help yourself, mate,' Daniel said, seeing Rhydian's eyes rest on the dish of sausages. 'Have what you like.'

Rhydian helped himself.

'So they're vegetarians,' Emma said, grinning, 'your foster parents?'

'Mmmm,' was all Rhydian could manage through a mouthful of sausage.

Finally, he sat back in his chair; full. He smiled at Maddy. 'It's got to be cool having a family you can be yourself around.'

Maddy was not going to praise her parents too much, not when they were staring at her. She nodded. 'Most of the time.'

'You're more than welcome here, any time,' Emma said to Rhydian. 'And if you've got any questions, just ask.'

'There is something,' Rhydian said. 'On the full

moon, when you change, do you do it in here, in the house?'

'Oh no, we have a secure room, in the cellar.'

'The cellar?'

Daniel stood up. 'We'll show you.'

Rhydian's eyes widened as he got his first glimpse of the room behind the heavily locked door. It was more like an animal's lair than a room and had been cut into the solid rock beneath the house. There were rock shelves to lie on, a mud floor and thick branches to claw.

'We call it the den,' Emma told him proudly. 'It's safe for us, and for everyone else.'

'But . . . but don't you ever want to just . . . run free?' Rhydian asked. 'Isn't that what being a Wolfblood's about?'

Emma shook her head. 'Being a Wolfblood's not just about giving in to our primal desires. It's also about being a responsible part of the community.'

'We have a rich heritage and culture,' Daniel added proudly. 'I've got books, if you'd like to read them. Romulus and Remus, founders of Rome, they were Wolfbloods. And Genghis Khan's tribe weren't called the Wolves for nothing.'

'But most of us agree it's better to tame our instincts,' Emma said.

Maddy looked surprised. 'Most of us?'

Emma realised she had said more than she intended. 'I just meant . . .'

'What, Mam? What did you mean? You always told me we all kept ourselves locked away.'

'I think you're wrong, Maddy,' Rhydian said. He turned to Emma. 'There are others that don't lock themselves away, aren't there?'

Emma looked at her daughter. 'We . . . we were going to tell you, after you transformed.'

'We didn't want to scare you,' Daniel added.

'Scare me?'

'There are Wolfbloods who don't share our values. Wild Wolfbloods. They're very rare. They hate humans and they're dangerous.'

'So it really wasn't you?' Maddy said to Rhydian. 'In Shannon's photo?'

'I told you it wasn't.'

'Then don't you see what this means?' said Maddy.

Rhydian shook his head.

'Tom and Shannon! They're out there, tonight!'

Daniel's face was usually cheery and full of good humour, but he suddenly looked anxious. 'What's going on?'

'Shannon took a picture,' Maddy said. 'I thought it was Rhydian. I didn't know about wild Wolfbloods. She's with Tom, looking for her beast of the moors.'

'Where? Where did they go?'

‘I could find it,’ Rhydian said. ‘I saw Shannon there yesterday.’

‘No, you two stay here.’ Emma turned to her husband. ‘Get the car, Dan.’

‘We’ll come with you,’ Maddy said.

‘No, Maddy, you stay here! Both of you! If there’s a wild Wolfblood out there, we’ll find it.’

Daniel and Emma were gone in seconds, but knowing their friends were in danger meant Maddy and Rhydian could not settle. ‘We’re not stopping here,’ Rhydian said after a few minutes. ‘I know where Tom and Shannon are. Your mum and dad are going by car but we can get there faster.’

Maddy nodded. ‘Yeah, but no wolfing out. Shannon’s got her camera.’

Six

Shannon had come into the woods prepared for a long wait. Equipped with a rucksack packed with pots, pans, plates and cutlery as well as a small camping stove and plenty of food, she met up with Tom and they settled at the site by the fallen tree trunk. Now she was preparing to cook beans, sausages and bacon by torchlight. Tom watched unenthusiastically, thinking he'd rather be at home watching the football with a packet of crisps.

The woodland was eerily silent and mist had started to settle. It was getting thicker by the minute. This was not Tom's idea of fun. A sudden rustling noise in the nearby bushes made him jump.

'What was that?'

'Over there,' Shannon said, 'in the bushes.'

She picked up her camera and began clicking off shots, the flash lighting up the area for a fleeting moment before the site was plunged back into darkness.

'It's just a badger, right?' Tom said nervously. 'Or a fox, maybe?'

'Sshhh,' Shannon said, peering into the mist.

There was another noise, and then what sounded like a growl. Shannon and Tom leapt to their feet. They stood back to back, trembling. Something was approaching.

'I don't think it's a badger,' Tom said nervously.

'And I think . . .' Shannon said, 'I think it's behind you?'

Tom spun around just as Jimi, Sam and Liam sprang from the mist, shouting and yelling. Shannon screamed.

Oh, your faces!' Jimi said, doubling up with laughter. 'Classic!'

'You . . . you . . .' Shannon stammered.

'Found your monster yet?'

Suddenly a wolf howl, loud and terrifyingly clear, cut through the night air.

The laughter stopped instantly.

'What was that?' Liam said.

'A dog,' Tom breathed. 'A . . . a big dog.'

'No,' Shannon said. 'It's the monster.'

Jimi looked terrified. 'I'm not stopping around to find out what it is.'

But there was no time to run. Something was hurtling towards them, at lightning speed, crashing through the woods and the mist. They stared, petrified, waiting, frozen to the spot.

And then Maddy and Rhydian came bursting into the clearing.

'You!' Shannon yelled. 'What are you doing here?'

'We . . . we thought we'd come and find you,' Maddy said limply. 'Didn't want you out here on your own.'

'We're hardly on our own, half the school's here now and . . .' Shannon stopped and peered into the mist. 'Look,' she breathed, raising her torch with a shaking hand.

They all turned to look. This time there was no mistaking the two golden eyes captured in the torch-light. A growl emerged from the mist.

Maddy knew for certain it was the wild Wolfblood. She turned to Rhydian. But he was gone. Shannon raised her camera and the flash illuminated the darkness. Another growl, louder and more ferocious, came from the mist.

'It is the monster,' Jimi breathed.

The eyes were moving closer. Maddy stepped to the front of the group so that her friends would not see her own eyes turn yellow and then gold. She would have to fight; there seemed no other choice. She had little chance against a wild Wolfblood but she might just give everyone time to escape.

But then, as they watched, there was a blur of movement through the trees. The eyes turned away and in the next second a ferocious battle had began. Howls and growls cut through the night.

'Rhydian,' Maddy whispered.

Shannon took another photograph. 'I've got to get this.'

But the flash of the camera brought the fighting to a halt and one set of eyes turned on them again.

'Run!' Maddy screamed, knowing that she had to try to get her friends to safety. And they ran, Maddy looking back all the time, hoping that Rhydian would follow. But the sounds of battle had begun again.

Suddenly Tom went sprawling. 'Ow!' he yelled.

Shannon and Maddy stopped but Jimi, Sam and Liam plunged on through the darkness.

'Help Tom,' Maddy yelled to Shannon.

'But what about you?'

'Give me your camera. The flash! It blinds the monster!' With the camera in one hand, she sped back towards the battleground.

Rhydian, in his wolf form, was fighting bravely but gradually losing. The wild Wolfblood was stronger and more skilful. As Rhydian staggered back, it closed for the kill, its teeth bared.

Then Maddy arrived. Now it was two against one. Maddy snarled, her eyes gold, as the wild Wolfblood came closer. Then she began flashing the camera, again and again, making the wild Wolfblood shy away in confusion and discomfort.

Maddy snarled loudly and Rhydian, rallied by her presence, let out a low growl. The wild Wolfblood had had enough. With a snarl of fury it turned away and disappeared into the forest.

As wolf-Rhydian slumped to the ground, panting heavily, Maddy began deleting the photographs she had taken.

'I have to leave Shannon something,' she murmured. She looked closer at another image. 'This one's just a shape; can't really see anything.' She turned to Rhydian, who was still in his wolf form. 'Help Shannon with Tom when you can; there's something I have to do.'

She leapt to her feet and sprinted away into the woods. Using her Wolfblood senses, it took her just minutes to track down Jimi and his mates. They heard footsteps behind them and then a loud, ferocious growl. And as they turned and screamed in terror, a blinding flash went off in their faces.

Rhydian was back in human form, doing as Maddy had instructed, helping Shannon with injured Tom.

'It was the beast, right?' Shannon said. 'It had to be.'

'Probably foxes,' Rhydian answered weakly. 'They really go for it when they fight.'

He was exhausted, barely able to speak, so he was doubly relieved as Maddy came running up.

'Where have you been?' Shannon asked.

'Looking for you guys.'

She smiled at Rhydian, thankful that the darkness hid the signs of battle on his face. As they neared the edge of the wood they heard a vehicle pull to a standstill and seconds later, Maddy's parents were hurrying towards them.

Shannon looked mystified. 'What are you doing here?'

'We, er . . . we came to find Maddy,' Emma said.

'Tom's hurt his ankle,' Maddy said, spotting her mum's angry glare.

Daniel helped Tom to the car as Emma went to Rhydian. 'We told you to stay in the house. You shouldn't have brought my daughter into danger.'

Rhydian didn't reply; he didn't the have the strength.

Back at the house the mood was quiet and subdued. Emma made them all hot chocolate while Rhydian dabbed the cuts and scratches on his face with a wet flannel. He saw Tom staring at him. 'Ran into a thorn bush,' he said quickly.

Shannon was checking the photos on her camera, surprised and dismayed that not one had a good image of her monster. 'I can't believe it. I took so many and they're all useless, nothing but mist and odd shapes.'

She came to the one Maddy had saved. 'That's not bad,' Maddy said. 'You can definitely see something. Maybe it's good enough for another poster.'

Shannon shook her head. 'I'm finished with posters.'

Maddy smiled. She took the camera and scrolled on a few more shots until she found what she was looking for, an image of Jimi, Liam and Sam, backing away, eyes wide with terror. 'What about this one?' she said, handing the camera to Shannon. 'Don't you think that'd make a good poster?'

Shannon laughed. 'Oh yes! Brilliant! I'll put copies up all over school tomorrow. And I've got the perfect caption to go with it – CRY BABIES OF THE MOORS – PROOF AT LAST!'

Seven

The Year 9 art exhibition promised to be a highlight of the school year. Students had been working at developing their themes and ideas for weeks and the opening of The 21st Century Family Art Show had drawn a big crowd of parents and friends.

Pupils had mounted their own displays, giving their personal take on what family meant to them in the twenty-first century.

'We are very proud of our students' work and I'm sure you will be, too,' Miss Fitzgerald said proudly as she wound up her welcoming speech.

Applause rang around the hall, but as students and visitors began circulating not everyone looked happy.

Rhydian's display featured just a single drawing. It showed a boy sitting alone, head bowed, in the corner of a room. When Maddy saw the drawing and went to speak to him about it he brushed her off and hurried from the room. Rhydian reckoned he didn't need family.

Tom was different. He was no great artist but he was a good photographer and an even better footballer. His display was entirely photographic: Tom in footballing action or being presented with trophies or medals. And his dad, looking on proudly, was in many of the photographs. Tom was desperately hoping that his dad would make it to the exhibition. Tom and his dad had always been great mates, but life had changed over the past couple of years. Tom's parents had split up and his dad had a new partner and a baby. It meant that Tom saw a lot less of him, but he'd promised to come tonight.

Jimi Chen's dad was staring at his son's display and didn't look impressed. Art was far from Jimi's favourite subject but he had tried his best. He always wanted to impress his dad but felt he could never live up to his expectations. Tonight was no exception. Jimi had completed a large oil painting of his dad standing outside a grand house; something like the house they lived in. It wasn't good, Jimi knew that, but he was hoping his dad might at least praise him for trying. He didn't. After a long, cold stare he shook his head and turned away.

He walked over to Tom's display, where Maddy and her parents were standing.

'Very inventive, Tom,' Mr Chen said, smiling appreciatively at Tom's photographs. He pointed at a picture of Tom receiving a trophy. 'Was that when you were Player of the Year?'

Tom nodded, while across the room, Jimi could not

hide the hurt, disappointment and fury he was feeling.

As Mr Chen walked on, Tom checked his watch.

'Your mum not coming, Tom?' Maddy's mum, Emma, asked.

'No, she's working late. But Dad will be here soon, he promised.'

There was a huge range of work at the impressive exhibition, everything from pottery, to wood sculptures and textiles. The Three Ks, unsurprisingly, had mostly centred their displays on fashion.

And Kara, the most artistic of the three, had been especially inventive, using ultraviolet ink for her paintings. The inks were stacked to one side, as part of the display, and to reveal the finished work, visitors had to pass an ultraviolet lamp across the surface of the painting.

The evening wound on and gradually visitors drifted away. Maddy's parents were among the last to leave. Trailing behind them, Maddy glanced towards a window and saw Rhydian outside, staring through the glass at her. She was distracted for a moment and when she looked again he was gone.

On their way out, Maddy and her parents passed Tom, sitting dejectedly by his display.

'Is your dad still not here?' Maddy asked.

Before he could answer, Tom's phone beeped, signalling a text had arrived. He read it quickly. 'Dad's . . . he's stuck in traffic. He'll be here soon.'

'Right,' Maddy's dad, Daniel, said. 'We're off, then. Have a great weekend, Tom.'

Tom smiled, trying his best to look bright. 'Yeah, see you.'

Half an hour later it was all over. Mr Jeffries, as head of Year 9, was the last to leave the building. As he walked towards the main exit he noticed that a light was still on in the exhibition. He went quickly into the hall and switched it off.

As he turned away a figure moved from behind one of the displays and crept noiselessly across the room.

The hand-written sign taped to the double doors gave a clear instruction: DO NOT ENTER!

'What's happened?' Maddy, Shannon and Tom were peering through the small windows on Monday morning.

'Someone's trashed the place!' Shannon said. 'All that work.'

'All that mess!'

The Three Ks arrived and instantly decided that one little sign was not going to keep them out. They pushed their way through the gathering crowd and swept into the hall. Maddy and the others followed.

They were met with a scene of total devastation; paintings and photographs ripped from frames and torn into pieces, sculptures shattered, ink bottles smashed, splinters of glass lay everywhere. A whole term's work was destroyed.

More and more pupils, including Rhydian, were arriving. Maddy could see that most were visibly upset, but Rhydian just shrugged as if he didn't care a bit.

Mr Jeffries came hurrying in. 'No one is supposed to be in here!' He was about to order everyone out but saw how disappointed and upset everyone was. 'Just don't touch anything,' he said much more gently.

'What happened, sir?' Maddy asked.

'Someone came back here on Friday night, after the exhibition closed,' he told them.

'What about the security cameras?' Shannon asked.

Mr Jeffries shook his head. 'All we have is a glimpse of someone running away, very quickly. In the dark, it could be anyone. But you all know the rules, we have a zero-tolerance policy towards vandalism, and if school property is treated disrespectfully then privileges are withdrawn. I've just been speaking with the head; the end-of-term disco is cancelled.'

The mood of silent dejection turned instantly to shouts of protest.

'Oh, sir!' Kay yelled.

Kara was even louder. 'You can't do that!'

'Unless!' Mr Jeffries was loudest of all and the students fell silent again. 'Unless the vandal is found,' he continued. 'So if any of you know anything, I suggest you come and speak to me very soon.'

Eight

The rumours started instantly and spread like wildfire. Everyone had a theory; everyone had a view. Possible suspects were identified and probable motives were considered. The vandal had to be found, the end-of-term disco was one of the biggest events of the year.

The hunt swept through Year 9 and soon the entire school was on the lookout for the culprit. Wild allegations were made, most very quickly rejected.

Then Jimi Chen reminded a few carefully selected and gossipy listeners that Rhydian Morris was said to have trashed the photographic darkroom on his very first day at the school. His friends had done their best to hush up the incident, but in a place like Bradlington High School nothing stayed secret for very long.

Rhydian immediately went from possible culprit to prime suspect. In most people's eyes he was most definitely guilty.

Rhydian knew about this new development as quickly as anyone. Whispers and mutterings would stop as he approached, but a Wolfblood could hear distant conversation and voices long before they were hushed.

Maddy heard the whispers too and she was worried. She'd seen Rhydian outside the hall just before she'd left the exhibition with her parents. She didn't want to believe the worst, but the doubts were there in her mind.

Then at the beginning of the lunchtime break, as Rhydian was crossing the playground, Jimi shouted, 'Hey, Leek Boy, is it true you smashed up the darkroom on your first day?'

Rhydian stopped. 'I knocked some stuff over, that's all.'

The Three Ks were on hand to continue the inquiry. 'Where were you on Friday night, Rhydian?' Katrina asked.

'None of your business.'

Kay spoke up next. 'If you're innocent, why not tell us?'

'I can tell you where he was because I saw him,' Jimi said loudly, ensuring everyone heard. 'He was hanging around the playground, in the dark.'

'Is that true?' Kara said accusingly.

Rhydian could feel his temper rising. He had to get away, quickly. He turned and walked off and Maddy followed.

'Hands,' she murmured urgently.

Rhydian looked down. The veins in his hands had turned silver. He had to stay calm. 'You think it was me as well, don't you?'

'Was it?'

'No! It was not!'

'But I know you were there, I saw you at the window.'

'Yeah, I came back and I saw you with your parents.'

'Why didn't you come in?'

'Because I'm just . . .' He stopped walking. 'I'm just not ready for all that family stuff.'

Maddy nodded. 'I believe you.'

'Yeah, well, it doesn't matter much anyway, I'll still get blamed.'

'Not if we find the person who really did it.'

Maddy sought out Shannon and Tom, who were sitting together in the darkroom. 'We can't stand by while the wrong person is accused,' she told them.

'If he is the wrong person,' Tom muttered.

Maddy looked closely at her friend. He'd been moody and distant all day, nothing like his usual cheery self.

Shannon, though, was already making a plan of action. She got up. 'Come on, we need to take another look at the scene of the crime,' she said, leading the way.

'But why?' Tom asked grumpily as he trailed after her.

'If we can work out *why* someone did it, then we can work out *who* did it.'

'Yeah, right, Sherlock Holmes.'

'Look, Tom, I believe Rhydian, Maddy said. 'And Shannon's right, we need evidence.'

The hall was still a scene of devastation. Shannon moved around stealthily, taking photos on her phone, looking closely at damaged displays. 'If one person's display has been particularly picked on, that could mean the vandal has a grudge against them.'

Maddy was looking at Kara's work, or what remained of it. The ultraviolet painting lay on the floor, a smashed ink bottle close by. But the display didn't look any more damaged than most of the rest.

'Look!' Shannon said suddenly. She was standing by Tom's display board. Every one of his photographs had been ripped off and torn into tiny pieces. The vandal had obviously spent most of his time and energy here.

'Tom,' Shannon asked, 'have you fallen out with someone recently?'

'No!' Tom snapped defensively.

Maddy and Shannon exchanged a look.

'What's wrong, Tom?' Maddy said.

'Nothing.'

'Is it your dad? Did you argue on Friday?'

'No!'

'Tom, I know something's happened.'

Tom sighed. 'We didn't fight. He didn't even turn up. I got a text saying he couldn't make it. He's been calling all weekend but I told Mum I wouldn't speak to him.'

'But why didn't he turn up?' Shannon asked.

'What does it matter? He let me down. Again!'

Maddy had rarely, if ever, seen Tom look and sound so gloomy. And not just gloomy, she thought, as he avoided her eyes, but guilty too.

Rhydian was summoned to Mr Jeffries' office during the first lesson after lunch. As he left the room he glanced towards Jimi Chen, who was grinning broadly. Rhydian was in no doubt; Jimi had dropped him in it.

Maddy waited for a couple of minutes before sticking up a hand and asking if she could go to the toilet, feigning nausea. She did feel sick; sick with worry that Rhydian would lose his temper and wolf out if Mr Jeffries' questioning wound him up.

She hurtled from the classroom and up to the head of year's office on the first floor. Crouching by the door and engaging her Wolfblood hearing she could hear every word being said in the room. And it was apparent that tempers were already rising.

'Look, Rhydian, I'm trying to get to the truth here. You're telling me you went home and then came back to the exhibition and then went home again. And you walked here? From Stoneybridge?'

'Don't call me a liar!'

Rhydian put his hands down by his sides, hoping that Mr Jeffries would not see them. The veins were already turning silver.

Maddy knew she had to do something. 'Rhydian,' she whispered, knowing that Rhydian's Wolfblood hearing would be engaged. 'You have to calm down.'

Rhydian heard the words but he was struggling to do as Maddy instructed. 'You can't just accuse me!' he said to Mr Jeffries. 'I didn't do it.'

'I'm simply asking you to explain exactly where you were and why.'

Maddy whispered again. 'Deep breathing, Rhydian, stay calm. Think of lying in a green field, in the sun.'

Maddy's words of advice made Rhydian laugh out loud, he couldn't stop himself. But it didn't go down well with Mr Jeffries. 'What's the joke, Rhydian? You are seriously trying my patience.'

Rhydian let out a slow breath. The laughter had helped, broken the tension and taken away his anger. He was back in control.

'Last chance, Rhydian,' Mr Jeffries said. 'What happened on Friday night?'

'I came back to school on my own and Maddy's parents gave me a lift home.'

Mr Jeffries considered Rhydian's words, while on the other side of the door Maddy was furiously scrolling through her phone contacts to dial her mum's mobile.

'Right,' she heard Mr Jeffries say, 'I'll call Mrs Smith now.'

'Yeah, call her,' Rhydian said. 'She'll back me up.'

She did. Maddy just about managed to get through to her mum and whisper a few hurried words of explanation before the landline in the farmhouse rang. She hoped that her mum would cover for them, knowing that she considered Rhydian part of her Wolfblood pack – and she was right. Emma told Mr Jeffries that they had indeed given Rhydian a lift home.

A few minutes later, Rhydian left the office and returned to class with a smile on his face. Maddy was already there, and she was smiling too.

Only Jimi Chen looked unhappy.

Nine

Shannon had been doing a lot of thinking, and not much of it concerned her schoolwork. She took Maddy and Rhydian aside before last lesson and said a single word. 'Ultraviolet!'

'Ultraviolet?' Rhydian repeated, hoping for a bit more explanation.

'Yes, remember Kara's ultraviolet painting? The ink was everywhere in the hall; the vandal must have trodden in it.'

Rhydian grasped where Shannon's thoughts were heading. 'And they won't have washed it off.'

Shannon nodded. 'Because it's ultraviolet and they don't know it's there.'

'Right!' Maddy said excitedly. 'But how do we check everyone's shoes?'

'I'll show you,' Shannon said, marching quickly away.

As students went to their lockers to grab coats or collect bags at the end of the day, Shannon was already there, running the ultraviolet lamp over their shoes.

Most of Year 9 were accustomed to Shannon's eccentric ways, but if anyone asked exactly what she was doing she had a cover story ready; she was operating a dog-poo detector. After that they were mostly happy to raise their shoes for inspection.

Maddy and Rhydian stood watching as Tom came down the corridor. Maddy had been hoping they'd find the culprit before Tom appeared. All day she'd had this nagging fear that he might just have gone on the rampage in the hall after being let down by his dad. But he was one of her best friends; she couldn't bear the thought of his guilt being exposed in the glare of an ultraviolet light.

She went quickly to him. 'Tom, we need to talk about what really happened on Friday night.'

'What?'

'I know you were still in the hall when we left. What happened after that?'

Tom could hardly believe what Maddy was saying. 'You're kidding me! You really think I'd do that, to other people's work?'

'I want to help, Tom.'

Tom took the ultraviolet light from Shannon and handed it to Maddy. 'Go ahead, then, check!'

Maddy had no option now. Tom lifted one foot and she ran the lamp over his shoe. Nothing. It was the same with second shoe. 'Tom, I'm . . .'

'Thanks, Mads,' Tom said, walking away, furious. 'Some friend you are.'

Tom had another shock in store outside school. He'd been expecting his mum to pick him up that day but his dad stood waiting by his parked car.

'It's all right, Tom,' he said, 'your mum knows I'm here.'

'No, it's not all right, Dad. You let me down the other night, again. You said there wouldn't be any emergencies this time.'

Both Tom's parents were doctors and his dad was frequently on emergency call. 'It wasn't a hospital emergency, Tom, it was a family emergency.'

'Oh, your precious new baby again, eh?'

'Tom, please let me explain.'

But Tom wasn't staying around for explanations. 'Don't bother. And I'll make my own way home.'

Maddy was approaching Tom and his dad as she saw Tom hurry away. She stopped to speak to Mr Okanawe, who obviously wanted to explain.

'I was trying to tell him, Maddy,' he said. 'There was an emergency with the baby. She was ill, really ill, I had to get her to hospital. I didn't want to let Tom down but I had no choice.'

Maddy nodded. 'Let me speak to him, Mr Okanawe. Please?'

'But I don't even know where he's gone.'

'I'll find him.'

Tom was sitting on a bench on the far side of the school grounds. He looked up as Maddy approached but said nothing.

'I'm so sorry, Tom,' Maddy said, sitting next to him on the bench. 'I shouldn't have accused you.'

'No, you shouldn't.'

'I jumped to stupid conclusions.'

'Yeah.'

'Can you . . . can you forgive me?'

Tom shrugged. He hated falling out with his friends, especially Maddy, and at that moment he really needed a good friend. 'I guess.'

They sat in silence for a few moments.

'I spoke to your dad,' Maddy said eventually. 'Your little sister was ill.'

'Half-sister. All he ever talks about is Grace. Grace can smile; Grace can crawl. I never wanted a half-sister, all I want is my dad.'

'But if he'd come to you instead of getting her to hospital and something had happened . . .'

'I know. And I don't want anything bad to happen to Grace, it's just that . . . I need him too, Mads.'

Maddy nodded. 'I think he knows that. Give him

another chance, eh, Tom? Like you're giving me another chance.'

Shannon looked as disappointed as she felt. The ultraviolet search had not revealed the vandal.

'You didn't check everyone,' Rhydian said, trying to console her. 'We'll give it another go tomorrow.'

'Yeah, tomorrow,' Shannon said dejectedly. They were on their way out of school when she realised the ultraviolet lamp was still in her hands. 'Oh, I should have put this back.'

'It's all right, I'll do it,' Rhydian said.

'Do you mind? Really? I'll miss my bus otherwise.'

'It's no problem, honest.'

He took the lamp and was passing the Year 9 lockers when he saw a brand-new pair of shoes, tied together by their laces, hanging down from an open door.

More out of impulse than because he expected to see anything, Rhydian stopped and ran the lamp over the shoes. Then he stared. The shoes were unmistakeably splattered with blobs of ultraviolet ink. Then a hand reached around the locker door, removed the shoes and put them in the locker. The door swung shut and Jimi Chen stood there, startled to see Rhydian staring accusingly at him. 'Push off, Leek Boy,' he said and hurried away.

Rhydian grinned, ready to move at Wolfblood speed.

Jimi rushed through the main school doors, looking back to see if he was being followed. Then he came to a sudden jolting halt. Rhydian was already outside.

'I just want to know why you did it,' Rhydian said in a low voice. 'Why would you want to destroy everyone's work?'

'Get lost!'

Jimi ran back into school, sprinting to another exit at the rear of the main building. But when he burst through the doors, Rhydian was there. Again. 'Did you do all that damage just to get me into trouble?' he said to Jimi.

The truth was out. Jimi knew it, but he couldn't stand there and admit it to Rhydian. He ran into school again, but just as before, when he crashed through the main doors Rhydian was waiting for him. 'You've had it in for me ever since I got here. You told Jeffries it was me, didn't you?'

Jimi was close to tears. 'You think everything is about you! Poor little orphan boy! You don't know how lucky you are. No one telling you you're not good enough; that you're a disappointment. That's what I get all the time.'

Rhydian glanced to one side for a moment and then back at Jimi. 'Next time you lose your temper, smash up your own things, not other people's.' Then he walked away.

'Off to find Jeffries, are you?' Jimi yelled after him. 'Gonna tell him it was me, and that I . . .'

The words froze on Jimi's lips as his dad stepped into view from the side of the building. He'd heard everything. 'He won't need to tell Mr Jeffries anything, Jimi,' he said coldly. 'You'll tell him.'

Tom had taken Maddy's words of advice to heart and had made things up with his dad. They were talking together and Maddy had joined them, when Rhydian arrived to explain what had happened with Jimi and his father.

A few minutes later, Tom and Mr Okanawe drove away. Maddy and Rhydian could see Tom chattingly animatedly and his dad laughing.

'I'm glad they sorted it out,' Maddy said.

'Families, eh?' Rhydian said. 'Maybe I'm the lucky one, being on my own.'

Maddy smiled at him. 'But you're not on your own.'

Ten

Everyone thought Jimi Chen would be expelled when the truth about the art exhibition vandalism was revealed, but the fact that he owned up was taken into consideration and he was let off with a suspension and a severe warning that for any future incidents the police would have to be involved.

He returned to school for the start of the Year 9 exams week and was soon heard telling his mates that he wished the suspension could have lasted for a further seven days.

The upcoming exams meant stress and worries for many students, including Tom. He was dyslexic and although he was allowed added time for written exams he was really worried about the English test.

Shannon, as always, was determined to do well in every subject and had been revising like crazy. Even Kara, the brightest member of the Three Ks, was displaying exam concerns, much to the surprise and dismay of Kay and Katrina. They rarely thought about exams and never about revision.

Maddy was especially worried. She'd been struggling

with her revision for days and was feeling unwell. There was a raging headache that wouldn't go away, her limbs were throbbing, her teeth and gums hurt and she was finding it almost impossible to focus.

Only that morning her mum had realised what was happening. 'You're on the brink of transforming. You'll have to stay at home; you won't be able to cope with a week of exams.'

'No way, Mam,' Maddy snapped, not for the first time. She'd been irritable for days, often close to losing her temper. 'I've worked hard for these exams, I'll be all right.'

Emma wasn't so sure, but she knew how important the exams were to her daughter, so agreed to let her go to school. Before Maddy left, Emma went to the kitchen cupboard and retrieved a small bottle of purple liquid. She gave it to her.

'What is it?'

'It's a Wolfblood rescue remedy. Just herbs, but it'll keep you calm. Put a couple of drops under your tongue if you feel stressed.'

Maddy felt stressed from the moment she arrived at school. Just walking across the playground and being jostled by noisy, shouting kids set her nerves jangling.

Then Tom came running up. 'Hey, Mads, what happened?'

'Sorry?'

'Last night, you never showed up.'

Maddy stared blankly.

'Last night, Mads, English revision?'

'Oh, Tom,' Maddy said, remembering. 'Things got a bit hectic at home. But English isn't till tomorrow, we could revise in the lunch hour if you like?'

Tom nodded. 'Cool.'

He had his football kit bag with him and as he swung it on to one shoulder it thumped into Maddy's school bag. She felt the crunch and when she looked down saw a purple stain spreading over the front of the canvas bag. Opening the bag for a closer inspection she was hit by an almost overpowering smell of woodland herbs. 'Oh, great,' she muttered.

The first exam was maths, scheduled for immediately after the lunch break. Somehow, Maddy had to get through the morning. It was going to be difficult. When Mr Jeffries called her name in registration she couldn't stop herself from shouting an irritated reply. 'What!'

Her form teacher gave her a long, cold stare.

'Sorry, sir.'

Rhydian, sitting next to her, had realised what was going on. 'Hot flushes?' he whispered.

Maddy nodded.

'Shooting pains through the body?'

She nodded again.

'Jaw and teeth hurt?'

She nodded for a third time.

'Mmmm, could be an interesting day.'

'Shut up!'

'*Maddy!*' Mr Jeffries said.

'Sorry, sir,' Maddy moaned again.

The morning passed agonisingly slowly and by the time the lunchtime bell sounded Maddy felt ready to burst. 'I don't think I can stand this much more,' she told Rhydian.

'You know what helps?'

'Tell me, please!'

They were in the playground. Rhydian began to jog backwards and Maddy had to jog to stay with him.

'The best way to get through the pre-transformation blues is to . . . *move*!'

As he yelled the final word he turned and sprinted away across the playing field. Maddy hesitated but then she was sprinting too, hoping that no one had spotted them racing away at such high speed. She had to run, she had to burn off the wild energy coursing through her veins. Rhydian dashed through a gap in the school fence and Maddy followed. Then they were in the surrounding woodland, running free, like young wolves.

The dining hall was a blur of movement and noise. In the middle of it all Shannon sat at a table, seemingly unaware of the chaos all around her as she concentrated on her revision.

The Three Ks were queuing for their lunch. Kay and Katrina were exchanging the latest school gossip, but Kara was glancing towards Shannon.

Tom was scanning the hall, searching for Maddy. When he saw no sign of her he strolled to the queue, joining Jimi Chen and his mates.

'Seen Maddy?' Tom asked.

Jimi grinned. 'Took off with Leek Boy, last I saw.'

'You mean Rhydian?'

'Need your little girlfriend for English revision, do you?'

'Whatever, Jimi,' Tom said, moving away and trying to hide his disappointment. Instead of revising with him, Maddy had gone off with Rhydian. As Tom left the dining hall he almost collided with the Three Ks, who were weaving their way through the tables with lunch trays.

Kara stopped at the table where Shannon sat. 'Hey, Shan.'

Kay and Katrina looked mystified. 'Kara, what are you doing?' Kay asked.

Kara ignored her and spoke to Shannon. 'Do you mind if I sit down?'

Shannon was too stunned to answer immediately. She glanced around the room. There were plenty of empty tables, but for some unknown reason Kara wanted to sit with her.

'Is this a wind-up?'

'No, really, it's not.'

'Actually, Kara, I'm trying to do a bit of revision.'

'I know,' Kara said, sitting at the table. 'And I thought we might revise together.'

'I can't believe this is happening,' Katrina said to Kay as they tottered away.

Rhydian and Maddy had finally collapsed down on to the leaf litter somewhere in the middle of the woods. They were both panting. Maddy was weary but elated. Burning off her pent-up energy had made her feel much better.

'Thanks,' she said at last. 'I know I've got Mam and Dad but it's really good to have someone of my age to share this stuff with.'

'Yeah, that goes for me too.'

'I've always hated keeping it from my friends.'

'Everyone has secrets. I bet Tom and Shannon don't tell you everything.'

'Yeah, but they don't have secrets like us.' Maddy sat up suddenly. 'Oh, no . . . *Tom*!'

'What?'

'I was meant to revise with him!' She checked her watch. 'And we have a maths exam in ten minutes!' She leapt to her feet. 'Rhydian!'

'You've got to calm down, Maddy.'

Maddy sprinted away and Rhydian stared up at the sky. 'I'll catch you up.'

By the time Maddy got back to school the lunch break was almost over. This time she jogged across the playing field, much more aware now that it was not a good idea to be seen moving at the sort of speed she could manage.

Tom was listlessly kicking a ball around as she came jogging up. 'Tom! I'm really sorry, I only just remembered.'

But Tom had run out of patience. 'It doesn't matter.'

'No, it does. I'll come over to yours tonight, OK?'

'Forget it, Maddy,' Tom said, shaking his head. 'I don't need your help.'

Kay and Katrina were waiting for Kara before afternoon registration.

'You want to tell us what that was all about?' Kay asked. 'I mean, come on, Kara, you sat with Shannon Kelly!'

Kara shrugged. 'So what?

'Like, it was Shannon Kelly!'

Kara sighed. 'Look, you know you two are my best friends but the thing is . . . I need Shannon Kelly.'

'Why?' Katrina asked, bewildered.

'Because I think . . .' She stopped, unsure of whether to go on.

'Come on, Kaz,' Katrina said. 'You can tell us anything.'

Kara took a deep breath. 'I think . . . I think I might be . . . good at science.'

Her friends looked horrified.

'Oh, come on,' Kara said quickly. 'Aren't you fed up with being labelled as total airheads?'

Kay and Katrina did not reply.

'I've known it for ages,' Kara continued. 'I just . . . like . . . *get* science, sometimes even before the Nerd Brigade. But I never, ever, put my hand up. And why shouldn't I put my hand up?'

Kay and Katrina both opened their mouths to speak, but neither could think of an answer to Kara's question.

Eleven

The room was silent, the atmosphere tense. Single desks spaced evenly apart were in neat rows, with an examination paper waiting to be turned over on each.

Maddy sat at a desk near the back of the room. Her head was pounding and she could hardly keep still. The stress was overwhelming, but the raw tension in every part of her body had nothing to do with exam nerves.

As the clock ticked down to the start time, the door swung open and Rhydian came sauntering in.

Miss Parish, the teacher overseeing the exam, sighed. 'Nice of you to turn up, Rhydian.'

A ripple of desultory laughter ran through the room as Rhydian took the last remaining desk, a little in front of Maddy.

'Settle down, everyone,' Miss Parish said. 'You have exactly one hour, starting . . . now.'

There was a rustle of paper and then complete silence as anxious eyes scanned the examination questions. Shannon was one of the first to start writing.

At the back of the room Maddy sat completely rigid, as though she were frozen. Her senses were suddenly painfully alive. The ticking of the clock was thunderous, the pens scratching across paper like torture. She tried to focus on the exam question but it was impossible. Looking down at her hands on the desk, she saw that her veins had started to thicken and pulse.

She pushed back her chair and the screeching sound on the floor almost made her scream in agony. She looked down again and saw the dark silvery liquid flowing into the veins in her hands. It was happening, she was transforming. But it couldn't happen, not now, it mustn't. Close to panic, she deliberately dropped her pen and dipped beneath the desk to retrieve it, trying to hide her hands. But she had no idea what to do next and in desperation looked towards Rhydian for help. He was staring back at her and as their eyes met he nodded and then sprang to his feet. '*Fire!*'

Rhydian ran to the alarm on the wall and punched the glass with his fist. The fire alarm began to sound throughout the school. There were screams and cheers as students clattered from their desks and made for the doors and the corridor.

Maddy stayed under her desk.

'Walk!' yelled Miss Parish. 'Don't panic! Stay calm, everyone, please!'

Rhydian ran to Maddy and looked into her eyes. They were wide with terror. 'Maddy, it's over! Keep calm. Deep breaths, remember. Deep breaths.'

'Rhydian Morris!' Miss Parish's voice boomed from the doorway. 'You are in big trouble, young man.'

The entire school was mustered in the playground. Form teachers were checking registers to ensure that every student was present. If nothing else it had been a good test of the fire drill, but everyone knew there had been no fire.

Maddy was back to her normal self. The crisis had passed thanks to Rhydian's quick thinking. But not everyone appreciated what he had done. Shannon came storming over. 'You are mental, Rhydian Morris. Just because you want to waste your own time, doesn't mean you have to waste everyone else's.'

Then Mr Jeffries arrived. 'Rhydian, you come with me. The rest of the class will go to the form room to revise.'

Rhydian nodded glumly. 'Yes, sir.'

Mr Jeffries walked away and Rhydian followed.

'I can't believe he did that,' Shannon said, still furious.

'Shannon, why don't you back off a bit?' Maddy snapped, springing to Rhydian's defence.

'What?'

Maddy couldn't say what she desperately wanted to say, so she said nothing.

But Shannon was far from finished. 'And instead

of defending Rhydian, maybe you should think of your other friends a bit more. Like Tom. How many more times are you going to let him down, eh, Maddy?'

Maddy reacted furiously. 'Look, I know he's sensitive, but I've got a little bit more to deal with today than babysitting Tom! OK?'

Shannon stared, taken aback by her friend's outburst. Tom, talking nearby with a group of boys, heard the argument, like everyone else. He turned away in embarrassment.

The Three Ks, as always, had opinions to voice, but this time they were not speaking as one. 'He is mad, that Rhydian,' Kay said loudly.

'Totally,' Katrina agreed.

'He's not mad,' Kara said. 'He's just a rebel and he can't help it.'

'Oh, is that so?' Kay snapped. 'Well, you must be right, being as you're so clever. And you don't have to hang out with us, you know.'

'Yeah, go and hang out with your smarter friends,' Katrina added, 'if you think you're better than us.'

Kara sighed. 'D'you know what? I think I will.'

She walked over to Shannon. 'Hey, Shannon, what are you doing after school?'

'And why would you want to know that, Kara?' Shannon answered shortly.

'I thought maybe we could revise together. Is that OK?'

Shannon looked at Maddy, waiting for a response. But Maddy stayed silent.

'You know what, Kara,' Shannon said, smiling. 'It is OK. How about we head over to the science lab?'

Kara grinned. 'Great.'

'I don't understand you, Rhydian,' Mr Jeffries said, fixing Rhydian with his sternest stare. 'Sometimes you seem to be making a real effort to fit in and be part of the school, and then you spoil all the good work by doing something stupid, like today's prank.' He raised his eyebrows, waiting for Rhydian's reply.

'Yes, sir.'

'Yes, sir? Is that it? Nothing else to say?'

Rhydian had been trying to work out something to say on the way to the office, but had failed to come up with any believable excuse. 'I, er . . . I just sort of panicked, sir.'

'Panicked? You mean you had a panic attack?'

Rhydian almost smiled. Jeffries had given him the perfect excuse. 'Yes, sir, exactly, it was a panic attack. And the numbers on the exam paper, they all started . . . swirling.'

'Swirling?' Mr Jeffries looked concerned; he took the welfare of his students seriously.

'Yes, sir, swirling, a lot of swirling,' Rhydian said, warming to the story.

'Has this happened before?'

'A few times, but today was the worst it's been.'

Mr Jeffries nodded slowly. 'Mmm, perhaps we should see about getting you assessed.'

Rhydian could hardly stop himself from laughing. He'd been assessed many times; once more wouldn't bother him in the slightest. 'Yes, sir, maybe that would be a good idea.'

'But that doesn't mean you're off the hook. I'm putting you in detention for setting off the alarm.'

Rhydian nodded. A detention was no big deal. 'Yes, sir.'

Twelve

At the end of the day Maddy walked dejectedly to the darkroom, the place she had shared great times with Shannon and Tom. She wanted to wait to see Rhydian when his detention was over. She felt hurt about Shannon going off with Kara, and Tom leaving without speaking to her, but she wasn't really surprised. She'd given her best friends a hard time; what else could she expect? She wanted so much to explain to them what was going on, but that was impossible and always would be.

Maddy pushed open the darkroom door and saw Tom seated at a laptop, going through some photographs. And Jimi Chen was with him.

'What is *he* doing here?' Maddy said to Tom.

'I'm showing him some photos. You got a problem with that?'

'Yes, I do; he's not a member of the club.'

'Oh, and you've never let in anyone who's not a member?'

'That's not the point.'

Jimi grinned, got up from his chair and walked to the door. 'I think you two need some time alone.'

Tom kept his eyes on the computer screen, trying to blank Maddy out so that she too would leave.

She didn't. 'So what's with letting him in here?'

'It's none of your business.'

'Tom!'

Tom swung around. 'No, Mads! Do I ask you about everything you do?'

'Pretty much, yeah.'

'But you don't tell me everything! You've been weird since Rhydian arrived here, and you know it.'

Maddy was suddenly defensive. 'I . . . I don't know what you're talking about.'

'Look, I'm not stupid, Maddy. And neither is Shannon!'

'What do you . . .?' Maddy stopped, knowing that continuing the argument would only lead into deeper and more dangerous waters. 'Fine! I'll leave you to it, then.'

Shannon and Kara had been working steadily on their revision notes when Kara suddenly spotted bottles of chemicals on one of the science lab workbenches.

'Hey, Shannon, look.' She got to her feet. 'They must have forgotten to lock this stuff away after the fire alarm. Let's do some real science.'

'I . . . I'm not sure we should . . .'

But Kara was already checking through the chemicals. She fetched a Bunsen burner and various glass jars and test tubes from a cupboard. 'We can create a chemical reaction with this lot.'

'If we get caught . . .'

'Oh, don't panic, Shannon, it'll be fine. I'll do it if you won't.'

Shannon hesitated; it would be interesting to try an experiment. 'Let's do it.'

Soon they were working side by side, so engrossed in the work they didn't even notice Maddy when she arrived. Having failed miserably with Tom she'd decided to try to patch things up with Shannon. 'Hey, Shan?' she called from the doorway.

A bright purple flame crackled in a test tube.

'Wow!' Kara said. 'Amazing!'

Shannon still hadn't noticed Maddy. 'And *that* is a chemical reaction,' she announced proudly.

Maddy tried again. 'Shan, d'you feel like getting a hot chocolate at Bernie's when you're done?'

'Sorry, what?' Shannon said, barely glancing towards Maddy.

Kara was thrilled at the scientific success and was rummaging through the chemicals to see what they might try next. 'Can we do it again with an accelerant?'

'I don't think you should be doing that,' Maddy said. 'What is wrong with you all today?'

Shannon spun around and glared. 'Maddy, you're the one who's weird today!'

'Oh, ignore her,' Kara said. 'Let's just get on.'

But Maddy's fragile temper was rising too. 'Look, Shannon, once your new friend has got what she's after she won't want to know you any more. You do realise that, don't you?'

'Yes, Maddy,' Shannon replied coldly, 'I do realise that perfectly well, thank you.'

'What?' Kara said, looking highly put out.

'Oh, give it a rest,' Shannon snapped, suddenly realising that what she and Kara had been doing was not only dangerous; it was stupid. 'Actually, Kara, I'm not sure about this, so please put the chemicals down.'

'Right, I will!' Kara snarled, slamming down the jars she was holding and spilling chemicals on to the workbench and floor. 'If that's how you feel . . .'

'It is!' Shannon snarled back before turning her anger on Maddy. 'And you've been a cow all day. To Tom, to me, to anyone stupid enough to care about you.'

'You have no idea about my day!'

'I'm out of here!' Kara yelled. She furiously pulled on her coat and it brushed against a test tube, which wobbled and then crashed to the floor.

'Yeah, and me too!' Maddy said, following Kara through the door.

Shannon was left standing among the broken glass and spilt chemicals. 'Aren't you going to help me clear up?' she yelled after them.

There was no reply. Shannon sighed and began searching for cloths or paper towels to clean up the mess. She didn't notice the mingling chemicals on the workbench start to fizz. And as she got to her knees to mop up the liquid on the floor a thin stream of vapour rose into the air.

A minute later the door opened; Maddy had returned. 'Shan, I'm sorry, I shouldn't have said that and I . . .'

She stopped. Her Wolfblood senses were signalling danger. But before she could move, the chemicals on the bench ignited and a flash of flame shot upwards. Startled by the noise, Shannon instinctively jumped back, cracking her head on the corner of the workbench. She slumped to the floor, unconscious.

'Shan!' Maddy yelled as the blue chemical flame crackled and spat.

Maddy's eyes widened. She drew back; fire meant fear for both wolves and Wolfbloods. Somehow she made herself cross to the fire alarm and smash the glass. But as the alarm sounded, her natural Wolfblood defences took over. She dropped on to all fours, her eyes turning yellow, the veins in her hands and neck beginning to darken and throb. She was starting to transform. A loud wolf howl echoed through the lab.

Rhydian had just finished his detention. He heard the alarm but his Wolfblood hearing also picked up and located the howl. 'Maddy,' he breathed, and he began to run.

Bursting through the lab door he instantly saw Maddy battling to stop a complete transformation. 'We have to help Shannon,' she screamed. But Rhydian was equally terrified of the fire. He stood transfixed, staring at the flames.

'Get help!' Maddy yelled, realising that Rhydian could not come nearer. 'Rhydian, get help!'

Rhydian nodded, his eyes still fixed on the fire. Then he turned and hurtled from the room. Maddy was on her own. Fighting back the fear and summoning strength from deep within, she moved towards Shannon and the flames.

Shannon was starting to come round. She was still terribly dazed and her eyes were streaming from the chemical vapour, but as she peered through the smoky haze she saw Maddy coming towards her. But it wasn't Maddy; it was like Maddy but . . . but . . . It was unbelievable. It couldn't be. It was impossible.

'No,' Shannon muttered. And then she passed out again.

Maddy had almost made it to her friend. She could hardly breathe in the thick, cloying atmosphere and as she reached out to Shannon she was suddenly completely overcome by the fumes.

Tom was outside the darkroom with no idea where the fire was located. Then Rhydian came tearing down the corridor. 'Did you do this?' Tom yelled. 'Twice in one day!'

'No! There really is a fire, in the lab! It's Maddy . . . and Shannon and . . .'

Tom looked horrified. 'I'll go! Find Jeffries, he'll still be here!'

Smoke was pouring from the open lab door as Mr Jeffries ran down the corridor, a fire extinguisher in his hands. Rhydian was just behind him.

'Stay here!' the teacher ordered as they reached the lab. He peered into the acrid smoke and coughed as the fumes hit the back of his throat. He could see nothing for a moment but then he glimpsed movement. Someone was edging towards the doorway.

It was Tom. Tom, with a scarf wrapped around his head and covering his mouth and nose. Maddy was with him and together they were hauling the barely conscious Shannon to safety. Losing consciousness had caused Maddy to return to her human form, just before Tom reached them, when she'd come round again.

'Tom!' Mr Jeffries yelled. 'Tom, thank heavens!'

As the three friends squeezed through the doorway

and sank on to the corridor floor Mr Jeffries plunged forward with the fire extinguisher, quickly dousing the flames.

Rhydian went to Tom. 'You saved them, Tom! You saved them!'

Coughing and spluttering, Shannon sucked in huge, desperately needed gulps of air. Her eyes were red raw, like Maddy's.

'It's all right,' Tom told her gently. 'It's over now. You're safe, Shan, you're safe.'

Shannon wiped her eyes and then stared at Maddy, a look of disbelief on her face as she remembered what she had seen. Or what she believed she had seen.

'Are you all right, Shan?' Maddy gasped from the other side of the corridor.

Shannon could not reply. She just stared. And stared.

Thirteen

Tom was hailed throughout the school as a hero, something he found a bit embarrassing, although he was secretly pleased. Shannon and Kara were given a severe reprimand by the head for dabbling with chemicals in the lab and Maddy got through the remainder of exam week by using plenty of the Wolfblood rescue remedy her mum provided.

But the drama in the science lab brought more than a sore throat and stinging eyes for Shannon. It also brought a total belief that she had seen something happen to Maddy during the fire; that in some inexplicable way, she'd become inhuman. And Shannon was convinced that Rhydian knew Maddy's secret.

She told Tom about everything she had seen and what she believed, but he brushed it off, saying the fumes and smoke had caused her to hallucinate. Tom had his own concerns regarding Maddy and Rhydian; he suspected they were dating. And he didn't like that, secretly thinking that if anyone was dating Maddy, it should be him.

Everyone had been looking forward to the school field trip. The visit to the island of Lindisfarne had been organised for just after exam week. The remote island was steeped in both history and mystery and could only be accessed by a stone causeway, which was completely under water at high tide.

Mr Jeffries was an expert on the medieval history of Lindisfarne and had even written a book on it. He was enjoying telling his students all about his research and writing as the minibus crossed the causeway.

When the vehicle came to a halt and the students piled out, Maddy and Rhydian, bursting with pent-up energy, started running and jumping around like a pair of six-year-olds.

There was a reason for this. That night there would be a full moon and the two young Wolfbloods were already hugely affected. And this full moon held even more significance for Maddy; this was the night she'd make her first complete transformation. Everything had been carefully planned and timed. On returning from Lindisfarne Maddy and Rhydian were to go straight to the Smiths' house so that they could be safely in the den with Maddy's parents before the moon rose in the night sky.

But as Maddy and Rhydian chased and scampered about on the shingle, the other students and the staff watching as though they were acting like a couple of infants, Shannon and Tom were watching more closely, for their own separate reasons.

Miss Fitzgerald was the second member of staff on the trip. 'Maddy, Rhydian! Come on, how old are you?'

'Yes, come on, everyone,' Mr Jeffries shouted. 'First stop, Lindisfarne Castle.'

When the group reached the castle they packed into a small, stone-walled room and Mr Jeffries began to give them the further benefit of his indisputable knowledge, going way back to the sixteenth century. 'Lindisfarne Castle was built around 1550 using stones from the abandoned monastery.'

It was all very interesting, if you were into monasteries and monks and raids by heavily armed invaders. But Maddy was already claustrophobic and Rhydian felt the same. They both needed to be outside. To be free and to run wild.

When Mr Jeffries took a breather and Miss Fitzgerald continued the story of monks hiding from bloodthirsty invaders, Maddy could take no more. She nudged her way through the crowd and, with Rhydian following, ran for the staircase leading up to the roof. Outside on the wide flat roof they both felt instantly better. The air was cool and clean and they could see for miles in every direction.

'That night in the cellar's not looking so good now, is it?' Rhydian said, breathing deeply. He had agreed to spend the night in the den with Maddy and her parents, mainly for his own safety. But he was not looking forward to it.

And neither was Maddy. 'It's going to be horrible. I don't know how my parents get through it, locked away like that, every full moon.'

The door to the stone stairway swung open. It was Tom, who had decided he didn't want Maddy and Rhydian out of sight for too long. 'You two are missing the best bits of the story. Monks getting their heads chopped off, it's brilliant stuff.'

Miss Fitzgerald had followed Tom up the stairs, and as she stepped on to the open roof it was clear that she didn't like heights. 'Maddy, I'm sorry if my story was a little too much for you?'

'No, it wasn't that, miss.'

'Claustrophobia,' Rhydian said. 'It got to me too.'

Tom raised an eyebrow. 'I didn't know claustrophobia was catching.'

After a tour of the island, Mr Jeffries set a task for the afternoon, and as the group huddled around the minibus, he handed out worksheets. 'The questions cover the castle, the limekilns, the church and priory, and the village. So for those of you who've been paying attention this should be very easy.'

The students split into small groups and Shannon made certain that she and Tom were with Maddy and Rhydian. 'We're sticking to them like glue,' she whispered to Tom.

'And remember, everyone,' Mr Jeffries added before they moved off, 'be back at the minibus by five o'clock without fail, or we'll miss the tide.'

The questions were not particularly difficult, especially for students like Shannon, who devoured history and fascinating facts. The foursome went back to the castle, quickly found the answers to the questions set there and then headed towards the priory. Shannon studied the worksheet as she walked. 'So now we need to answer four questions around the village and priory, two in the limekilns and two on the beach.'

Maddy and Rhydian were still bursting with energy. 'Right,' Rhydian said, spotting an opportunity to get away, 'you and Tom take the priory and the village and we'll do the rest. Sorted.'

'Hang on,' Tom said. 'We're a team; we're not meant to split up.'

'All that matters is getting the answers, Tom. Let's just get it over with.'

'Then we can meet up for ice cream,' Maddy added quickly.

'Brilliant idea,' Rhydian said, 'meet you at the village later, then.'

'But . . .' Shannon and Tom said together.

But before they could argue further Maddy and Rhydian had hurried away. Shannon sighed. 'I'm sure Rhydian knows the truth about Maddy.'

'Oh, don't start that werewolf stuff again.'

'I know what I saw in the science lab, Tom! Look, have you heard of Occam's razor?'

Tom shrugged his shoulders. 'Is that the one with the swivel head and four blades?'

'No! It's a scientific principle. It says that the simplest explanation is always right, even if it sounds crazy.'

'You're off your head, Shan! Maddy and Rhydian are dating, that's why they're spending so much time together.'

'Tom, they're cousins, they can't be dating.'

'Distant cousins, they might as well not be related at all.'

'We'll, they're related enough for him to know her secret. Look, we've both got a theory, what we need is evidence. They got away from us this time, but they won't again. From now on we don't let them out of our sight. Agreed?'

Tom nodded. 'Agreed.'

* * *

As soon as Maddy and Rhydian were certain they were out of Tom and Shannon's sight, they started to run, quickly, but not as quickly and freely as they wanted. That was too dangerous during the day.

They made for the beach and were soon splashing happily along the tideline.

Rhydian stared out at the sea. 'This would be a brilliant place to spend full moon. Safe on an island, running on the beach and in the ruins.'

'Yeah,' Maddy answered, 'it would be amazing.'

'So let's do it!'

'Rhydian, we can't. My parents are expecting us home.'

'To share that cosy little den.'

'Look, I should be with my family for my first transformation, and you promised you'd be there too, so there's nothing more to talk about. Come on, race you!'

They darted further along the beach, forgetting completely about the worksheet questions. Eventually they came to a long row of boat sheds where Jimi Chen and his mates, Liam and Sam, were lurking.

A scowl crossed Jimi's face as he spotted Rhydian. The memory of Rhydian revealing the truth about the trashing of the art exhibition still festered in Jimi's mind.

As Rhydian nodded a friendly hello and went to walk by, Jimi reached out and yanked his rucksack from his shoulder. Rhydian didn't bother to react to the pathetic gesture. Jimi hesitated for a moment and then hurled the rucksack up on to the nearest boat-shed roof.

'Go get it, Leek Boy,' he said, grinning.

The sheds were unusual, like wooden boats turned upside down, so the roof was curved and hull-shaped. A narrow ridge ran the full length at the top. Rhydian's rucksack was hooked over the highest end of the ridge and would not be easy to reach.

But Rhydian's spirits were high and he was bursting with energy. With Maddy and the others watching he climbed on to the roof at its lowest point and then began walking up the ridge, like a tightrope walker.

'Be careful, Rhydian,' Maddy called, 'it's dangerous.'

Rhydian had no sense of danger as he moved closer to the high point of the ridge. He stopped, staring out towards the rolling waves, then threw his head back to feel the salty sea breeze on his face. But as he took a step forward he slipped and went tumbling down the side of the shed. He landed on the shingle and let out a yell of pain.

'My ankle,' he moaned as Maddy ran to him.

Even Jimi looked concerned. He reached down to help Rhydian to his feet.

'No, don't move him,' Maddy said quickly. 'He could have broken it. I'll stay here, you go and get help.'

For once Jimi didn't argue. He nodded and then ran, with his two friends trailing behind as usual.

Fourteen

Mr Jeffries and Jimi were helping Rhydian very carefully towards the minibus. Mr Jeffries looked outwardly calm, but he was worried. A check had revealed that no bones seemed to be broken, but Rhydian said his ankle was still hurting badly. It was slow progress.

'What about the tide, sir?' Rhydian asked, sensing the teacher's anxiety. 'We won't be able to get off the island.'

'We'll get off,' Mr Jeffries answered, a lot more confidently than he felt. 'I told you all to be back at the bus fifteen minutes early. We should still make it.'

They finally reached the minibus and scrambled aboard, and with Miss Fitzgerald at the wheel the vehicle sped away towards the causeway.

But they were too late. The barrier was down, the causeway was closed and a notice stated that the next low tide was not until midnight. They were stuck on the island. In the minibus, there were groans of dismay and moans of complaint.

Maddy was desperately worried. The full moon was approaching and with it her first transformation; and there was nothing she could do to prevent that from happening. But she noticed that Rhydian did not seem to share her fear; he was smiling as he glanced towards the seashore.

Miss Fitzgerald turned the minibus around and drove to the nearby Lindisfarne Hotel in the village, where Mr Jeffries telephoned the school while students made calls home. The only realistic decision was quickly confirmed – they would stay overnight at the hotel and leave the island as soon as the morning tide allowed.

'Think of it as an added adventure,' Mr Jeffries told the group, 'although you're going to have to squeeze in three or four to a room.'

Maddy had found somewhere quiet to speak on the phone to her mum. 'Rhydian can hardly walk and Shannon is totally certain I'm the beast of Stoneybridge Moor. She won't leave my side. What are we gonna do, Mam?'

'Don't panic,' Emma told her. 'Rhydian will be fine once he transforms; the full moon heals almost anything in a Wolfblood. But you must both be out of the village before full moon.'

'And how do we do that?'

'You've got to think your way out of it, Maddy; we can't help you now. But whatever you do, make sure you get out of the village in time.'

Rooms were being allocated and as Rhydian could not climb the stairs, he was to bed down in what was actually a ground-floor storage room. There was just space to put up a camp bed but Rhydian was quite content. He would be alone in the room, and that meant it would be easier to get out unnoticed later.

Maddy was hoping that she too would be given a single room but her hopes were dashed when she was put in with the Three Ks. And as soon as the Ks spotted that the room had one enormous king-size bed and one single mattress on the floor, they claimed the bed. Maddy had the mattress.

Shannon was disappointed not to be in with her best friend, but she wasn't going to let that stop her from keeping a close watch on Maddy, even if it meant staying awake all night.

The group had an early dinner and afterwards, when they gathered in the lounge, Miss Fitzgerald came up with the idea of sharing a few ghost stories before bed. The lights were dimmed to add to the spooky atmosphere and Miss Fitzgerald told a story that she called 'The Ghost Dog of Lindisfarne'. She vividly described how, only the previous year, a young couple had gone to the abandoned limekilns after hearing a strange, unearthly howling.

'Little did they know,' Miss Fitzgerald said dramatically, 'that they were entering the lair of the ghostly white dog of Lindisfarne, and that they were never going to come out.'

'I wish I could get out now,' Rhydian whispered to Maddy. 'How will you manage it?'

'Shannon's hardly taken her eyes off me, but as far as she knows I'll be with the Ks,' Maddy said quietly. 'But I'll tell them I'm moving in with Shannon, they'll be delighted. Then I'll come down and help you get out.'

Rhydian was momentarily confused. 'Help me? Oh, you mean my leg.'

'Mam says it'll heal when you transform.'

'Don't worry about my leg; I'll manage. We'll meet at the boat sheds.'

Miss Fitzgerald was finishing her story. 'And all they found was a mobile phone with a voice recording of terrible screams and a dog snarling. Officially the case remains unsolved; unofficially they blamed the white dog of Lindisfarne.'

The Three Ks shivered and exchanged frightened looks, while Jimi Chen loudly claimed that he didn't believe a word of it.

Miss Fitzgerald just laughed. 'Anyone else have a story to share?'

'I do,' Shannon said quickly.

'Great, let's hear it, then, Shannon.'

Shannon looked directly at Maddy as she started her

tale. 'On the moors above Stoneybridge, something roams. Something that on the night of full moon, is seized by impulses it can't control and it becomes a beast!'

A chorus of groans echoed around the room.

'All right, quieten down, everyone,' Mr Jeffries said. 'Let Shannon tell her story, although I think we may all have heard it before.'

Maddy was waiting by the boat sheds when she heard someone running. She peered around the corner of the building and saw Rhydian hurtling towards her. He grinned broadly as he came to a halt.

'What happened to your limp?'

'Oh, yeah, the limp,' Rhydian said guiltily.

'You fell off that roof deliberately,' Maddy said, realising the truth. 'I can't believe it; you didn't hurt yourself at all! You knew I wanted to be with my family and you ruined it!'

'Look, I had to be here tonight, it's a special place.' Rhydian could see that Maddy was hurt and upset. 'Yeah, all right, it was stupid. But you know what it's like, the instinct to run free. I just think it's wrong to lock ourselves up at full moon.'

Maddy sighed. 'Maybe you're right. And at least we both managed to get out in time. I had to tell Shannon to back off when she followed me into the toilets, and then I had to run up to the Ks and tell them I was moving in with Shannon. At least they were glad to see me go, but I hate lying to Shannon.'

'I guess it was easier for me,' Rhydian said, 'being on the ground floor.'

'Yeah,' Maddy said, managing a smile. 'And specially as there's nothing wrong with your leg. Come on, let's go.'

Rhydian had come closer than he knew to being apprehended. Tom was lurking nearby and as Rhydian slipped out of the hotel, he went to follow. But at that moment Mr Jeffries emerged from the lounge and stopped Tom from going anywhere.

By the time Tom and Shannon got together they both knew that they had been outsmarted.

But Shannon had no intention of giving up her quest to discover the truth. 'I'm going to find them, and this time I'll get some answers. You coming?'

'Oh yes.'

Fifteen

Rhydian and Maddy were standing together on the beach. Small waves broke gently on the shoreline as the moment Maddy had been nervously anticipating for so long approached. The excitement was building in her chest.

The clouds parted and a first sliver of pale moonlight shone down on them. In an instant all her fears and nervousness had gone. Maddy looked at Rhydian and they both smiled before lifting their faces to the rising moon.

It happened swiftly and naturally. The veins in Maddy's hands pulsed and turned silver and the change spread quickly up her arms into her neck and through her entire body. Her eyes turned gold and her blood began to flow dark silver.

She dropped on to all fours and then quickly the transformation was complete. Wolf-Maddy gazed in wonder at her changed body, marvelling at her paws and her swishing tail. Her golden eyes flicked to the right and she saw wolf-Rhydian at her side, preening himself in the moonlight.

Wolf-Maddy raised her head and howled at the moon.

Tom and Shannon were hurrying by torchlight through the quiet main street in the village when they heard the long, echoing howl.

Tom stopped dead. 'The ghost dog. The one Miss Fitzgerald was telling us about.'

'That was no ghost,' Shannon breathed. 'And no dog.'

She pointed at the full moon hanging huge in the night sky.

'Full moon,' she said. 'Maddy's changed.'

'You're . . . you're kidding, right, Shan?'

A second howl, longer and deeper, cut through the still night air.

'She's on the beach, Tom. Let's go.'

The two transformed Wolfbloods were running side by side across the shingle and sand, moving like lightning towards a rocky outcrop, which led inland to the ancient abandoned limekilns. Soon they were padding into the archways, alert and inquisitive, instinct telling them to explore and discover.

Wolf-Maddy howled again and this time the sound was different as it bounced off the ancient walls and echoed into the shadows. Wolf-Rhydian howled too, deep and longer, like before.

The two young Wolfbloods padded around, pawing

the ground, delighting in their freedom and moving a little further into the limekilns. And then suddenly they both turned their heads and stared out into the night. Torchlight flicked across the ground, coming nearer. There were voices too. There was no time to dash outside without being spotted, so the Wolfbloods scurried away, going deeper into the maze of rock tunnels.

Tom and Shannon arrived at the arched entrance a few moments later.

'Nothing here,' Tom said nervously, without even looking and anxious to get away. 'We might as well go.'

But Shannon was on her knees, her torch pointed at the ground. 'Look at this.'

Tom moved closer and stared down. In the dust was a large, perfectly shaped paw print.

'That's not a dog, Tom,' Shannon said. She shone her torch into the tunnels. 'We're going in.'

Tom swallowed, his mouth dry. 'Do we have to?'

'Yes, we do.'

The network of brick and stone tunnels wound deep into the ground. But there was only one way out, so the Wolfbloods had to use all their cunning and stealth to avoid being spotted by their pursuers.

Torchlight flashed and flickered against the bricks and stone and more than once almost caught wolf-

Maddy or wolf-Rhydian in its beam. They were trying to work their way back to the entrance, staying together, scampering quickly away from the light, and turning back when they sensed the way in front was blocked.

But then wolf-Maddy moved a little ahead. Shannon thought she heard a sound and ran towards it, with Tom following. The Wolfbloods were separated and as wolf-Maddy scurried down a tunnel she came to a dead end. She was trapped, with no way out. No escape. The torchlight flashed from one side of the tunnel to the other as wolf-Maddy cowered in the darkness and Shannon and Tom came nearer and nearer.

Shannon sensed they were closing in on their target. 'We've got her now, Tom,' she whispered. 'I know we have.'

Suddenly something cannoned into Tom from behind. He went sprawling, crashing into Shannon, sending the torch she held flying from her hands. Momentarily wolf-Maddy's tail was captured in the beam.

'There!' Shannon screamed. 'There!'

Wolf-Maddy crouched back in the inky darkness, knowing that wolf-Rhydian had knocked Tom to the ground and was waiting for her. As Shannon scrambled for her torch wolf-Maddy ran forward and took a giant leap over both her friends, and as she landed her tail flicked across Tom's face.

'It's the ghost dog!' he yelled.

Shannon had found her torch. She jumped to her feet and shone the beam along the tunnel. But they were gone.

'There are no such thing as ghosts, Tom,' she said. 'It was Maddy.'

Mr Jeffries and Miss Fitzgerald were rousing the students early; they would not miss another tide.

Tom and Shannon were both already up. They'd agreed when wearily returning to the hotel that they would meet first thing to confront Rhydian. They at least knew where he was, or was meant to be.

Shannon led the way to the ground-floor storeroom and knocked on the door. After a few moments it opened slowly and Rhydian stood there rubbing his eyes, still half asleep.

Shannon came straight to the point. 'Where were you last night?'

'What?'

'Maddy was out all night. We followed the sound of howling to the limekilns and there was something there.'

'What?' Rhydian said again. 'Look, what's this got to do with me?'

'I think . . . I think Maddy changed last night, became something else. And you knew about it; you were with her.'

Rhydian was desperately trying to come up with a believable explanation but he was still groggy from the transformation. 'What are you talking about? This is mad.'

'Something knocked Tom over, and it wasn't human.'

'Then how should I know what it was? A dog? A fox? Local kids? Could have been anything.'

'Where was Maddy all night?'

Rhydian shrugged. 'Why don't you ask her?'

'Fine! I will!'

Shannon went stalking away, this time with both Tom and Rhydian in tow. She stormed up to the Three Ks' room, where Maddy was meant to have spent the night, and banged furiously on the door. 'Open up!'

'Go away, loser!' came a voice from inside.

'I'm coming in!' Shannon pushed open the door and barged in. The Three Ks were still under the duvet, but there was no sign of Maddy.

'Exactly as I expected.' Shannon turned back to Rhydian, ready to continue her interrogation. Then a door at the end of the landing opened and Maddy emerged, carrying a pillow and a folded-up duvet. 'Oh,' Shannon said, suddenly deflated, 'there you are.'

'Yeah, here I am,' Maddy said more brightly than she felt. 'You didn't think I was going to share with those three, did you? I sneaked downstairs and spent the night on the sofa.'

'But . . . but . . .'

Shannon was speechless but Tom managed a question. 'But you did go out, didn't you? Shannon couldn't find you.'

'Yeah, me and Rhydian went for a walk. His leg was hurting and he said walking made it feel better.'

'And I would have told you that,' Rhydian said to Shannon, 'if you'd given me a chance to explain.'

'Mmm,' Maddy said, smiling, 'I can smell bacon. 'You lot coming for breakfast?'

'Yeah!' Rhydian answered. 'I could eat a whole pig!'

Maddy dumped the pillow and duvet and hurried down the stairs, followed by Rhydian. Tom looked at Shannon and shrugged his shoulders, and then he, too, headed downstairs.

Shannon didn't move. She was thinking, turning over in her mind what she'd been told. She didn't believe it, not a word. But she would get to the truth; she was more determined than ever.

Sixteen

Maddy's first transformation meant that the rebellious side of her nature was fully unleashed and for a while it became difficult to keep under control.

It wasn't completely unexpected; at least not by Maddy's parents or Rhydian. They had all gone through the same experience after their own first transformations. But it caused Maddy problems at home and at school.

The Wolfblood side of her being was wild and untameable and it began to dominate the human side. She went from sensible to show-off, from careful to careless and from thoughtful to thoughtless. She started dressing punk-style, with bright red hair and matching lipstick and black mascara, which did not go down well at home, or at school.

'Who dressed you this morning, Maddy?' Mr Jeffries asked in registration. 'Lady Gaga?'

But the new brash and brazen Maddy was quick with a put-down of her own. 'And who dressed you, sir? Your grandma?'

The comment shocked the rest of the class and

earned Maddy a detention, but it did nothing to dampen her new rebellious spirit. When Kay of the three Ks took part in a street dance demonstration in the hall, Maddy took delight in upstaging her by leaping on to the stage and proving she was a far better dancer, leaving Kay in tears.

This dramatic change in her personality and behaviour was bizarre and shocking to Tom, but only made Shannon ever more certain that her best friend was also the beast of Stoneybridge Moor. Proving it had become an obsession. Tom tried time and again to get Shannon to drop it but there was no way she would let go. She would look for signs, hunt for clues and wait for opportunities to demonstrate beyond any doubt that Maddy was something other than human.

Maddy and Rhydian both had an after-school detention. It was another case of Maddy pushing their form teacher too far and Rhydian trying to help, only to end up in trouble himself.

The hour was almost up and Mr Jeffries had left them alone in the room for a few minutes while he went to speak to the head teacher.

Maddy was bored, although for once her energy, like Rhydian's, was starting to run low. As always, their lives were dominated by the cycle of the moon and they were just one day away from the low point in the month for Wolfbloods. Just as full moon released their full Wolfblood powers and led to a transformation, the time of no moon saw their powers diminish to virtually nothing. Even their normal human strengths were reduced as they endured a period of extreme fatigue and a lack of energy.

But the full effects were still a day away. On a shelf behind Mr Jeffries' desk stood one of his proudest possessions – a large and highly polished trophy won a few years earlier in a history quiz.

Maddy got up from her chair, went to the shelf and took down the trophy. She smiled at Rhydian. 'Jeffries won't be back for five minutes; he told us. Let's live a bit while we've still got the chance.' Taking the trophy, she went to a window, opened it and began to climb out. She glanced back at Rhydian. 'You coming or what?'

Rhydian could not resist the challenge. Maddy led the way, sprinting across the playground and then climbing a fire escape to jump from one part of the building to another. She was heading for the sports hall, the tallest building in the school complex. But as she leapt on to the roof she stumbled and, scrambling to grab a hold, caught her free hand on a rough edge. She was cut, not badly, but the wound was bleeding.

Rhydian joined her on the roof and Maddy pointed to the place she had in mind for the trophy. 'Jeffries is always saying nothing gets past him in this school; let's see if he spots this.'

They were back at their desks when Mr Jeffries returned. He failed to even notice that the trophy was missing.

When Maddy woke up the following morning she felt grim. It had been similar to this before her first transformation but now the fatigue was much more extreme. Her parents looked and felt just as bad.

The cut on Maddy's hand was still seeping blood, so she hoped this might get her mum's sympathy. 'Can I stay home?'

'No.'

'But my hand's bleeding.'

'Put a plaster on it.'

'Oh, this is so unfair!'

'Look, Maddy, one day someone will notice that once a month, when there's no moon, you're away from school. And they'll want to know why. Shannon's already on your case, and Shannon's a bright girl. Just come home as soon as school's over because the closer it gets to nightfall, the worse you'll feel.'

'Oh, great, thanks.'

* * *

Maddy arrived at school feeling dreadful and one look at Rhydian, who was slumped against a wall looking totally washed out, confirmed that he was in an equally bad way.

'I didn't think you'd come in,' Maddy said.

'Tried to get out of it, but the Vaughans wouldn't have it. They said they're going out somewhere.'

Maddy groaned. 'Now I really know why my parents hate no-moon days so much.'

'Yeah, it's really tough.'

But they were about to experience a moment that would briefly lift their flagging spirits. They heard cheering and applause coming from the direction of the sports hall and rushed to see what was happening. On the roof, perched on top of a heating vent, was Mr Jeffries' trophy, and as he and other teachers watched and a crowd gathered, a workman was being hoisted in a safety crane to rescue it. As the crane came to a halt and the man retrieved the trophy he decided to play to the crowd, so he turned and victoriously raised the gleaming trophy above his head.

A huge cheer went up although Mr Jeffries did not look amused.

Rhydian leaned close to Maddy and whispered, 'Wolfbloods one, humans nil.'

* * *

First lesson was science and the topic was DNA. After explaining that the DNA of humans was over ninety-eight per cent the same as chimpanzees, Miss Parish asked the class to list the similarities and differences between the two species.

As they settled down to begin writing, Shannon looked directly at Maddy. 'I think there's a more interesting question. Given the DNA evidence, could someone live and act as a human but actually be a completely different species? What do you think, Maddy?'

Maddy was not going to be drawn into a debate. 'That's completely irrelevant to the task we've been given.'

'Yeah,' Rhydian added, looking to help Maddy, 'we're studying chimps, not aliens from planet Shannon.'

'I wasn't thinking of aliens,' Shannon said. She raised a hand to attract Miss Parish's attention.

'Yes, Shannon?'

'Is our blood the same as a chimp's, miss?'

'Not exactly the same, but for this task it's close enough to be called similar.'

The mention of blood made Maddy glance down at the cut on her hand. The plaster she had put on it that morning was dangling off and the wound was still bleeding slightly. She put up her other hand. 'Miss, have you got a plaster?'

'Yes, of course.'

Shannon suddenly lost interest in listing the similarities between chimps and humans as she watched Maddy drop the old plaster into a waste bin while Miss Parish took a fresh dressing from the first-aid kit. Shannon's eyes rested on the waste bin. The opportunity she had been waiting for had arrived.

It was lunchtime when Tom looked into the science lab and saw Shannon hovered over a microscope. 'What are you doing? Does Miss Parish know you're in here?'

'She thinks I'm reading this book about blood she gave me.' Shannon had taken Maddy's old plaster from the bin and scraped a drop of blood from it on to a microscope slide. As Tom watched she placed the slide on to the microscope. 'I'm checking out Maddy's blood, to prove she's a werewolf.'

'Oh, not again, Shannon!'

Shannon looked up. 'Show me your index finger.'

'What for?'

'Just do it, Tom, please?'

Tom warily lifted one hand and before he could pull away Shannon had grabbed it and pricked his finger with a pin. 'Ow!'

'Don't be a big baby.'

Shannon smeared the drop of Tom's blood on to

another slide and then put it under the microscope's lens.

'Yes,' she said excitedly as she looked at the slide.

'What?'

'Look for yourself. This one's your blood and . . .'

But before Tom could look at the samples Miss Parish walked into the room. 'What are you two doing?'

'Looking at blood, miss,' Shannon said.

'What blood?'

'I'm comparing Tom's to . . . to some I found on the moors.'

Miss Parish sighed. 'Is this about your famous beast? I don't appreciate being lied to, Shannon, you said you wanted to read.'

'Please just look, miss, it's totally different.'

The teacher hesitated for a moment but then came over to the microscope to compare the two samples.

'Well, obviously, whatever this second one came from has a wound of some kind.'

'A wound?'

'Yes. What we can see are red and white blood cells. The white corpuscles are rushing to the site of the wound to fight off infection.'

'But it is animal blood, right?'

'*You* said it was animal blood. You said you found it on the moors.'

'But can't you tell for certain? From looking?'

'No, Shannon, we can't. We don't have facilities to do that here. It would have to go to a specialist laboratory to be analysed properly.'

Seventeen

Miss Fitzgerald pointed an accusing finger at Rhydian. 'Do you see another side to Rhydian? A dark side that no one else sees? Look closely, everyone.'

The drama teacher was giving a dramatic opening to her lesson later that day. The rest of the class thought the performance hilarious, only Rhydian and Maddy were not smiling. The teacher spun around to Katrina. 'And what about you, Katrina, do you have a dark side?'

Katrina's brow furrowed as she considered for a few moments. 'What, like fake tan? Is that what you mean, miss?'

The rest of the class groaned as Miss Fitzgerald laughed and clapped her hands. 'Right, in pairs we'll try a Jekyll and a Hyde scenario. This is a mirror exercise where Dr Jekyll thinks he can control his dark side, Mr Hyde. But can he? Let's find out.'

There was a lot of hurried movement as students paired up. Shannon, as always, went to Maddy. Rhydian was not keen on drama and was hoping that he'd miss out on a partner but found himself face to face with Tom.

'And . . . begin!' Miss Fitzgerald said loudly.

Most of the class played it for fun, while some of those keener on drama took the activity more seriously. Rhydian hardly moved, barely bothering to respond to Tom's movements.

'Come on, Rhydian, put some effort into it,' Miss Fitzgerald said. 'You lead now, you're Hyde and you hate Jekyll. Make it hard for him to follow, you want to break free.'

Rhydian was low on energy and really should have been taking it easy just to get through the day, but he began to put more effort into the exercise with quick, jerking movements. Tom did his best to follow.

'More, Rhydian!' yelled Miss Fitzgerald, pleased that he was responding. 'Come on, more. Go! Unleash the beast!'

With other students shouting and yelling, Rhydian suddenly roared loudly and began leaping about wildly. But it was too much. His vision became blurred, he felt dizzy; the room was spinning. And then he passed out.

Rhydian was taken by ambulance to hospital, accompanied by a member of staff.

Maddy was worried; visits to hospital were bad news for Wolfbloods. Secrets could be revealed. And

Maddy was also feeling unwell; the day was taking its toll. She should have gone home, as her mum had instructed, but at the end of the school day she went to the hospital with Tom and Shannon to see how Rhydian was doing.

They got the news as soon as they arrived – from Tom's mum, who was a doctor at the hospital. Tom had texted her earlier to tell her that his friend was being brought in and she had already seen Rhydian.

'We're going to run some tests on Rhydian's blood,' Dr Okanawe said. 'Just routine, in case he has an infection.'

Maddy tried not to let the panic she was feeling show. 'Is that really necessary? Rhydian just overdid it a bit in our drama lesson.'

'It's probably nothing, but we should make sure.' The doctor looked more closely at Maddy. 'Are you all right? You look a bit pale yourself.'

'Oh, I'm fine. Could we see Rhydian, please?'

The doctor smiled. 'I don't see why not.' She led the way, with Maddy at her side and Tom and Shannon following.

'I so wish it was Maddy getting that blood test,' Shannon whispered to Tom as they walked.

'Shannon! You can't wish illness on your friends.'

'You know that's not what I mean.'

'This is your best friend you're talking about.'

'A best friend who's lying to us.'

'You don't know that,' objected Tom.

'I do!' Shannon said too loudly.

Tom's mum stopped and looked back. 'What are you two arguing about?'

'Nothing!' Tom and Shannon said together.

In the examination room, a nurse was preparing to take a sample of Rhydian's blood. 'All right?' Rhydian said to his friends as they filed in behind the doctor.

Tom and Shannon smiled and nodded but Rhydian instantly noticed the panic on Maddy's face.

She shook her head, trying not to let the others see, and Rhydian realised she was trying to tell him that he shouldn't have his blood taken. 'I feel fine now,' he said to Dr Okanawe. 'This is a waste of hospital resources.'

The doctor smiled. 'It's kind of you to be concerned but I think we can just about afford a blood test. Look, lots of people are scared of needles, Rhydian, but it's all in the mind. There's absolutely nothing to worry about.'

'No, I'm not worried, it's just that . . .'

But before Rhydian could say any more the nurse had gently eased the needle into his arm.

Maddy stared as dark red blood began to fill the syringe. She felt dizzy, as though her own blood was draining through her body into her feet, and just as Rhydian had done earlier, she fainted.

* * *

She came round in an isolation ward. As her eyes slowly adjusted she saw Dr Okanawe, wearing a surgical mask, looking down at her. 'Maddy?'

Maddy was still groggy and for a few moments had no idea where she was or what had happened.

'How are you feeling? Maddy?'

Her head began to clear and the memories returned. 'Why are you wearing a mask?'

'It's precautionary, just in case you and Rhydian have a virus that's catching. We'll have a better idea when we get the results of the blood tests.'

Maddy glanced across at the second bed in the room. Rhydian lay there looking at her. 'They've taken our blood, both of us.'

Fear gripped Maddy's chest.

'Where are your mum and dad, Maddy?' Dr Okanawe asked. 'I tried calling them but just got the answerphone.'

'Don't know,' Maddy said, although she knew exactly where her parents were. She knew they would both be in a deep sleep at home as the full effects of no-moon day took hold.

'Well, I'll be back soon,' the doctor said. 'Just try to relax for a little while until we get the results.'

But there was no way they could relax. Rhydian turned to Maddy the moment the doctor had left the room. ‘So what was all that shaking your head about? What’s going on?’

‘The blood tests, you idiot. They’ll see we’re not human, they’ll find out we’re Wolfbloods!’

‘Are you sure? Can they do that?’

‘Yes! Look, when I was seven, I skewered my foot with a garden fork. Mam and Dad couldn’t take me to hospital in case they did a blood test. I had to wait a whole day until some doctor in Scotland they knew drove down to see me.’

‘So what do we do now?’

‘Get our blood samples back. Swap them, destroy them. I don’t know, Rhydian.’

She went to get up from the bed but was struck by another dizzy spell and fell back. ‘Oh, I feel terrible. I wish I could talk to my mam!’

Eighteen

Shannon could hardly contain her excitement. 'This is gonna rock the world, Tom.' They were in the hospital canteen, nursing soft drinks.

'Who cares!' Tom snapped. 'There could be something seriously wrong with Maddy!'

'Yeah, like the fact that she's a werewolf. The blood test will prove it, you'll see.'

'And then what?'

'What d'you mean, and then what?'

'Well, let's just say by some miracle you're right. What d'you think will happen to Maddy then?'

'How should I know?'

'Well, I've got a pretty good idea. They'll cart her off somewhere for tests and we'll never see her again. Is that what you want?'

'No, of course not.'

'Then why don't you start behaving like a friend? That's what Maddy wants, Shan, she wants her best friend back. What is it that you want?'

Shannon did not hesitate. 'The truth, Tom, that's all I've wanted all along.'

They lapsed into an uneasy silence; both absorbed in their own thoughts. They didn't see Dr Okanawe approaching until she reached their table. She was carrying two sheets of paper. 'We've got your friends' blood results,' she said, 'and I have to say they are most unusual.'

Shannon glanced at Tom, trying to keep the look of triumph from her eyes.

'Are they related?' Dr Okanawe asked.

'They're cousins,' Shannon said.

'Distant cousins,' Tom added.

The doctor thought for a few moments. 'Well, let's go and speak to them.' She spotted Shannon's surprised look. 'Oh, there's no infection.' She led them from the canteen back to the isolation ward and this time Tom and Shannon walked side by side in complete silence.

Maddy and Rhydian were sitting up, which was as far as they'd managed to get. Maddy was terrified. The secret she'd kept for so many years was about to be revealed. Her whole life was about to change, as well as the lives of her parents and Rhydian.

Rhydian was staring at the floor, as though he couldn't face hearing what Dr Okanawe was about to say. 'Well, as I told Tom and Shannon, I was very surprised at the tests' results, but as you're distant cousins that might explain the coincidence.'

Rhydian looked up. 'Coincidence?'

The doctor nodded. 'You're both AB negative, and that's extremely rare.' She smiled. 'Apart from that, everything's normal. No virus and no infection.'

Maddy and Rhydian stared in genuine shock.

'What do you mean normal?' Shannon gasped, hardly believing what she was hearing.

'I mean, I'm very happy to tell you there's nothing wrong with your friends.'

'But . . . but are they full blood tests? I mean, can you tell if they're human?'

It was Dr Okanawe's turn to look shocked. 'Of course they're human,' she said, confused.'

'But . . .'

'Leave it, Shan!' Tom said.

'But I . . . I . . .'

Everyone was staring at Shannon. Suddenly tears welled in her eyes and she ran from the room.

Maddy found Shannon sitting on the floor, alone in the corridor. She glanced up as Maddy walked wearily over and sank down at her side.

'You must hate me,' Shannon said, fighting back more tears.

'I could never hate you, Shan. You're my best friend in the whole world.'

'You wouldn't say that if you knew everything I've said about you.'

Maddy laughed. 'What, that I'm your beast on the moors?'

'Tom told you?'

'He's a good friend to us both, Shan.'

'And I am such an idiot.'

'No you're not, and just because you're wrong about me doesn't mean you're wrong about the beast. You're a truth-hunter, Shan, and that's one of the things I love about you.'

Shannon sniffed loudly and smiled, then flung her arms around Maddy and squeezed her tightly. 'I'm so sorry.'

'You don't have to be sorry, Shan, honest. But I'm really tired now, and I need to go home.'

Tom and Rhydian were waiting at the main entrance, where Shannon started to apologise all over again.

'Forget it,' Rhydian said, 'it's been a weird day.'

'It's all right, Shan,' Tom added with a beaming smile, delighted that his two closest friends were reconciled.

As they went to leave, Maddy's phone began to ring. It was her mum. 'I'd best take this, I'll see you tomorrow.'

Maddy spoke to her mum for several minutes and by the time she ended the call Tom and Shannon had gone. But Rhydian was still waiting. 'Did you tell your mum they're wrong about our blood?' he said as Maddy approached.

'They're not wrong. But apparently when there's no moon all traces of the wolf in our blood vanishes.'

'So . . . so we went through all that worry for nothing?'

'Yes, Mam says we got lucky.' Maddy sighed. 'But I don't want to live like this any more, Rhydian. I've got my friends back and I want it to stay that way.'

'Meaning?'

'I'm going to keep my wolf-self locked away for a while, and stick to being human.' She took a deep breath. 'And I'd really like it if you could do the same.'

Rhydian stopped and glared at her and Maddy was certain he was going to refuse her request. But then he laughed. 'Yeah, why not. It'll make a nice change.'

Nineteen

Keeping her wolf-side locked away was to prove far more difficult than Maddy imagined when, soon after, the local newspaper ran a story on an outbreak of attacks on farm animals. And then Shannon called in at Bernie's café to find several hand-written posters about missing pets on the wall.

'Do you reckon it might be your beast on the prowl?' Bernie said when he saw her studying the posters.

Shannon turned and glared. 'So you know about the beast as well?'

Bernie smiled. 'I hear about most things. Anyway, the story in the paper can tell you exactly where these farm animals have been killed. It's all there; page five.'

Shannon took the top paper off the stack and began to turn the pages.

'And remember, if you read it, you buy it,' Bernie said.

Shannon bought the newspaper; she needed to know all the facts.

Since the incident in the hospital, Maddy had been giving plenty of time to both Tom and Shannon, trying to bring their friendship back to normal. She desperately wished she could take them into her confidence by sharing her great secret, and had twice come close to telling all. But she'd pulled back. Expecting her friends to keep the secret was too much; they could never understand.

At least they were doing normal things again. Shannon's parents were having a night away and had agreed to her hosting a sleepover for her friends. Maddy was first to arrive. She was suffering with a cold but wasn't going to let it spoil the evening.

'My family have officially left the building,' Shannon announced as she opened the front door.

Maddy grinned. 'Let the sleepover begin.' She was really looking forward to their night, which they had planned carefully. Tom was cooking burgers and then they were going to settle down to watch a couple of movies.

But Shannon had already revised the plans. 'Don't get mad, Mads,' she said when Maddy spotted the partly packed rucksack, 'but I thought we might spend the night on the moors.'

Maddy knew immediately where this was heading.

'It's back, Maddy,' Shannon said before her friend could protest. 'The beast. Pets have gone missing; farm animals attacked. And I know where I can find it, or I think I do.'

'But if there is a beast, and it's out there, what makes you think it's safe for us to go out?'

'Because we'll stick together, look out for each other. That's what friends do.'

Shannon's words were an obvious reminder to Maddy that she still had ground to make up in the friendship stakes. 'Look,' she said gently, 'I know how important this is to you . . .'

'You have no idea. Everyone thinks I'm the town weirdo.'

'They don't.'

'They do. Maddy! I have to see a psychiatrist.'

'What! Why?'

'Because of what I said about you! Mads, I need to know if there's something out there and that I'm not completely crazy.'

'Shannon, you're not crazy, because . . .'

'What?'

Once again Maddy found herself on the brink of confessing all to her best friend, but once again she stopped herself. 'Because . . . the beast is real, and we will try to find it tonight.'

Tom arrived a few minutes later. He came in carrying two huge bags of food and wearing a brand new and very smart jacket. 'Dad bought it for me, from Manchester,' he told Shannon. 'Pretty cool, eh?'

Shannon was already heading upstairs. 'Totally impractical, you'll have to change.'

'Change? But why?'

'Because you'll freeze. I'll find you something else.'

She disappeared into her parents' bedroom and Tom went into the kitchen to unpack the food he'd brought. Maddy came through to join him.

'What's wrong with Shannon?' Tom asked as he emptied the bags.

Maddy took a breath. 'We're going beast hunting tonight.'

Tom visibly sagged. 'What? No way. I'm tired of being outside in the dark and cold.'

'Tom, she needs this.'

'Yeah, and I need to cook and eat and chill in front of the TV. Like we said. That was the plan, Mads.'

'Tom, I said Shannon needs our support, OK?'

'Right!' Tom said, knowing exactly how determined Maddy could be. 'Fine, but I'm eating before we go.'

He went back to unpacking the shopping and Maddy suddenly noticed the huge bag of mince on the work surface. She laughed. 'How many are you cooking for?'

'I wasn't sure how much to get so I got one kilo – each!' He took off his new jacket, put on the cook's apron hanging on the back of the kitchen door and began making burgers. Maddy watched as he worked; glad to be sharing the moment. And suddenly the urge to confess her secret was there again. It might be easier with Tom; he was so easy-going and understanding.

'Tom, you know we've been true friends, like forever? And we are true friends, aren't we?'

'Of course we are.'

'And you tell true friends everything, right? I mean, even if it's shocking. A secret. Something you don't want anyone else to know?'

Tom stopped working but he didn't look at Maddy. 'Is this why you've been so off with me?'

'What?'

'Because you knew I fancied you?'

Maddy stared. 'What?'

'It was just a crush, Maddy!'

Now Maddy was confused, and as embarrassed as Tom. 'Yeah, yeah, I knew that!

'Oh, right, you knew, but you didn't say anything? So did I embarrass you?'

'No. No!'

'Or did you have . . . feelings too?'

Maddy could feel herself blushing furiously and she had no idea what to say. 'Feelings?'

'Yes, feelings?'

'No! Yes! No! I . . . I didn't give it a second thought.'

'Oh, great!'

Maddy was making it worse rather than better. They were both relieved to hear the doorbell ring. As Tom thumped the mince down on to a chopping board, Maddy hurtled away to open the door to Rhydian.

Spread out on the kitchen table was a large map, on which Shannon had marked where the attacks on animals had taken place. Maddy and Rhydian were studying the map while Tom made burgers before sliding them into a sizzling pan.

Maddy had managed to tell Rhydian about Shannon's latest plan as she let him in, and before Rhydian could protest, she had insisted they help their friend catch a glimpse of the beast.

Rhydian was not enthusiastic. 'Say there is a wild Wolfblood out there,' he whispered, 'and it's come foraging and can somehow mask its own scent. How does seeing it help Shannon?'

'Her family think she's crazy, seriously, and she's starting to think they may be right. We have to help her, even if it means one of us transforming to do it.'

'What?'

'I know, but . . .' Maddy stopped abruptly as Shannon appeared in the hall.

'Come on, you two, let's look at this map,' she said.

The markings on the map indicated a clear pattern of activity, forming a wide circle around the village of

Stoneybridge. 'It's clearly not feeding in the same place twice,' Shannon told them, 'but killing and moving on. So that means tonight we need to be somewhere around . . .' she pointed at the map, 'here! It's not that far.'

Maddy nodded and then sneezed loudly. As she reached into a pocket for a tissue, Rhydian made a vain attempt at getting them out of the trip. 'I don't think Maddy should be going out with a cold like that.'

'I'll be fine, Rhydian,' Maddy said.

Tom looked up from his burgers. 'You might not be.'

Maddy sneezed again. 'I will, I'll be fine.'

'It doesn't sound like it,' Rhydian said.

Maddy glared. 'Rhydian! Can I speak to you for a minute?'

Rhydian glanced at the others, shrugged his shoulders and followed Maddy into the living room. This time he made sure to speak first. 'What if it's out there and it attacks us?'

'Then we defend ourselves.'

'Yeah, right, as wolves, in front of our friends?'

'Maybe it's time they found out about me.'

'This isn't just about you, Maddy; it's all of us. Me, your mum and dad, all Wolfbloods.'

'But I want to live truthfully, I've had enough of lies,' Maddy said.

‘Oh, Maddy,’ Rhydian said. ‘Why do you think Wolfbloods have kept themselves hidden for hundreds of years? Even the wild ones? Because it’s human beings who wiped most of us out. Your dad told me that. Was he lying?’

Before Maddy could answer, Shannon came in with a tin and a glass of water. ‘This is all I could find for your cold,’ she said to Maddy. ‘It’s aconite, one of my mum’s homeopathic remedies.’ She took a pill from the tin. ‘Open.’

Maddy obediently opened her mouth and Shannon popped the pill into her mouth. She gave her the glass of water and the tin. ‘If that doesn’t work, take one more, can’t do any harm. I’ll help Tom with the burgers; we should go soon.’

Rhydian was ready to continue the argument as soon as Shannon was out of earshot. But as he turned back to Maddy he stared in surprise. Her eyes had turned gold.

‘Maddy!’

‘I’m hungry,’ Maddy said, ignoring Rhydian. ‘I need meat!’

She went to barge past but Rhydian grabbed her and held her back. ‘You can’t go in there!’

‘But I’m hungry!’

‘No, you can’t! You’ll give us away!’

As Maddy growled and struggled, Rhydian pulled

her to the stairs, bundled her up to the bathroom and pushed her inside.

'Let me go! I need meat!'

Rhydian closed the door and locked it. Then he took Maddy by the shoulders and turned her around so that she could see her reflection in the bathroom cabinet mirror.

'Look! Look! You're transforming.'

It was true. 'But I'm not doing it!' Maddy gasped as she saw her golden eyes and the veins pulsing in her face.

'You must be!'

'No! No, I swear!'

'Then what is . . .?' Rhydian suddenly realised what must have happened. 'The pill Shannon gave you! Aconite! It must have caused this! Like some sort of allergic reaction.'

'Rhydian, what do I do?' Maddy said, panicked.

'You wait in here! I've got an idea.'

Rhydian unlocked the door and cautiously peered out to the landing. It was deserted, so he crept out and turned back to Maddy. 'Lock it,' he called back in to her. He waited until he heard the key turn in the lock and then tiptoed along the landing. But passing the top of the stairs he glanced down and saw Tom and Shannon staring up at him.

'Rhydian, what's going on?' Shannon said. 'We heard shouting.'

'Like you were fighting,' Tom added.

'It's Maddy. I was coming to tell you, she's being sick. It's really bad. I think I should take her home.'

Shannon went to step on to the staircase.

'No, don't come up,' Rhydian said quickly. 'It's a bit gruesome in there. She's throwing up, temperature's gone mad, the lot.'

Tom did not look convinced. 'Since when were you a medical expert? My parents are doctors, let me look at her.'

'But I told you, she's being sick.'

'Right, then I'll take her home.'

'No, I will,' Rhydian said firmly.

'Why do you have to do it?'

'Because I said I would. Anyway, you're cooking.'

'Rhydian, why do you want to keep getting Maddy on her own? Why not just admit you fancy her?'

'Me? I don't. Look . . .'

'Boys!' Shannon said, interrupting. 'Can we please not argue? As soon as Maddy feels well enough . . .' She stopped and looked at Tom. 'Do you smell burning?'

The kitchen smoke alarm began to shriek.

'The burgers!' Tom yelled. 'Oh no, my burgers!'

He dashed away to the kitchen with Shannon in pursuit and Rhydian took his chance to hurry into Shannon's room, where he powered up her computer.

His fingers pounded the keyboard and he clicked on a link to a web page.

'Thistle root,' he whispered as he read. 'Where am I meant to get thistle root?'

He went back to the bathroom, knocking softly on the door until Maddy let him in. Her eyes were still golden and the veins were pulsing in her hands and neck.

'You'll have to get home on your own.'

'But why?'

'Aconite is also known as wolfsbane, and it's not good for us. Go home, the effect will wear off later. I'll make excuses and get Tom and Shannon away from the house.'

'But I'm hungry, I need meat!'

'Maddy, go home! Wait till you're certain we've gone and then go home!'

Twenty

The burgers were not completely ruined, at least not all of them. Tom was munching on a survivor as Rhydian walked into the kitchen. Shannon had lost her appetite and seemed close to losing her temper too. The evening was not going the way she had planned. She pulled on her coat and then tipped the burnt burgers into the bowl containing the rest of the uncooked mince.

'What are you doing?' Tom asked.

'Going beast hunting.'

'With burgers and mince?'

'It's bait! And don't worry; I can manage alone. You two can take Maddy home. It's clearly what you'd rather do, and what she'd prefer.'

'No!' Rhydian said emphatically. 'Maddy can get home on her own.'

'Oh, I'm sure she can. But this sickness thing came on conveniently quickly. It looks to me as though she'd rather have you two fighting over her than go beast hunting with me. So I'll leave you all to it.'

'Shan!' Tom said.

Shannon was not prepared to listen to any more, or to wait. She picked up the bowl and stormed out, slamming the back door as she went.

Rhydian and Tom looked at each other. 'Do you think she'll be all right on her own in the woods?' Tom asked. 'I mean if that thing we saw before is still out there.'

'No! She won't!'

Tom grabbed the jacket Shannon had found for him earlier while Rhydian ran for his own coat.

Maddy came down the stairs a few minutes later, her eyes glowing gold. She sniffed the air and inhaled the tantalising smell of burnt burger and raw mince. Her Wolfblood side craved meat and the craving needed to be satisfied. 'Meat,' she breathed.

She padded through to the kitchen and spotted the empty burger pan on the cooker. Snarling and drooling, she went to the fridge and yanked open the door. No meat. She went back to the cooker and glared down at the stove. A few fragments of burnt burger stuck to the side of the pan and in one swift move, Maddy wiped a finger around the pan and stuck it into her mouth.

It only increased the craving. '*I need meat.*'

Deep in the woods, Shannon was hurrying towards her target area and Rhydian and Tom were steadily catching up. Using his Wolfblood senses, Rhydian could have got to her much sooner, but that would have aroused Tom's suspicions.

And Tom was already suspicious of Rhydian, but for a different reason. 'Why do you keep trying to come between me and Maddy?'

'What?'

'Did you know that she fancies me?'

'Maddy doesn't fancy you.'

'So why act all jealous, then, like you have some sort of claim on her?'

'I don't, Tom.'

It was dark in the forest; moonlight struggled to pierce the thick canopy. Rhydian's eyes had adjusted quickly but Tom's had not. He failed to spot the tree root sticking up from the path, tripped and went sprawling to the ground. 'Ow! Ow!'

Rhydian stopped and waited, thinking that Tom was overdoing it a bit. 'What's wrong, Tom? You only fell over.'

'Yeah, into a bunch of thistles!' Tom grimaced as he sat up, pulling thistle spikes from his fingertips. 'Ow!'

'Oh, thistles,' Rhydian said. 'Really!'

He bent down to get a closer look as Tom got to his feet and brushed himself down. 'Rhydian, what are you doing?'

Rhydian stood up holding a thistle plant by its root. He pointed the spiky part towards Tom. 'A thistle's a good weapon. Just in case.'

A long howl cut through the woodland and they both turned and stared back in the direction of Shannon's house.

'It's behind us,' Tom breathed.

The craving for meat was too strong. Maddy, in her semi-transformed state, could not simply go home as Rhydian had ordered. She had to feed.

She stepped from the back door drooling and snarling as her Wolfblood senses picked up the lingering trail left by Shannon's bowl of cooked and raw meat.

It was the scent that made Maddy howl. She began to move, swiftly, silently, through the woods, hunting down her prey.

Shannon was walking quickly, the torchlight bouncing off the trees, casting looming shadows that flickered and then disappeared. But Shannon was unafraid; she didn't scare easily. Suddenly there were footsteps behind her, moving fast, very fast, and her heart began to pound. She turned around, ready to use the torch as a weapon when the beast attacked.

It wasn't the beast. The torchlight captured Tom and Rhydian in its beam.

'Did you hear that howl?' Tom asked immediately.

'Yes, I heard it. And I thought you two were taking Maddy home.'

'What and leave you to face the beast alone? What kind of friends do you think we are?'

'Seemed to me that you're Maddy's friends tonight.'

Rhydian was peering into the dark woodland, his senses heightened. There appeared to be no immediate danger, so he turned to Shannon. 'She really is ill; I think it was that pill you gave her. I checked on the tin, it's years past its use-by date.'

'So . . . so she wasn't faking it?'

'No! All she wanted was to be here for you.'

'Oh, now I feel terrible.'

'Yeah, well . . .'

'Look, can we concentrate on this beast for now?' Tom said. 'We did all hear a howl, you know.'

Shannon nodded. 'You're right. Follow me.'

She stalked away into the trees.

'Follow you?' Tom said, hurrying to keep up. 'It's probably following us.'

Rhydian held back, his Wolfblood senses fully engaged. He could sense Maddy, and she was getting closer.

The clearing looked to be the perfect place for a sighting of the beast, cloaked in darkness and surrounded on all sides by trees. In the centre was a large tree stump, the ideal spot for Shannon's bowl of meaty bait.

She put the bowl on the stump and stepped slowly back, retreating towards the edge of the clearing. The beam from her torch flicked over the fringing trees. 'Tom,' she whispered.

'What?' Tom whispered back.

'Tonight you'll see the beast. It's near, I know it is.'

'Right,' Tom breathed, a lot less enthusiastic about the prospect of an encounter with the beast than his friend.

Shannon switched off her torch and they stood together at the edge of the clearing. They waited.

'Where's Rhydian?' Shannon whispered.

Tom looked quickly around. 'I dunno. He was with us, and then –'

'Ssshh!'

They froze.

'Did you hear that?'

'Yes,' Tom whispered. 'Rhydian, is that you?

There was no reply.

Wolfbloods, like wolves, used cunning to patiently stalk their prey, waiting for precisely the right moment to make their attack, utilising speed, surprise and strength.

Maddy had chosen her moment. She was hurtling towards the clearing, her eyes blazing and her wolf-like teeth ready to bite.

Rhydian moved just as quickly, and as Maddy went to leap he thudded into her side with a perfect rugby tackle and they both went crashing to the ground. Then they were struggling, battling, fighting on the woodland floor.

Tom and Shannon heard the grunts and groans. They spun around and Shannon fumbled for a few seconds to switch on her torch and locate the struggle. Finally the beam settled on Maddy and Rhydian. They were sitting up. Maddy coughed and appeared to spit what looked like some sort of vegetable root from her mouth. Rhydian was grimacing and staring at the large thistle stuck into the palm of one hand.

'Oh, very funny!' Shannon snarled. 'You've scared the beast off now! And what are you doing here, Maddy? You're meant to be ill.'

Maddy sneezed and stood up slowly. Her eyes had returned to their normal colour, all traces of Wolfblood had disappeared. She spat another piece of root from her mouth. 'I didn't want to let you down.'

'But how did you know where we were?'

'I . . . I just guessed, from what you showed us on the map.'

Shannon's temper softened. 'I'm sorry, Mads, I thought you didn't want to come.'

'It doesn't matter,' Maddy said, removing the last bit of thistle root from between her teeth. 'It was that pill, it gave me a really weird reaction.'

Tom went over to the tree stump and picked up the bowl. 'Can we go now?'

Back at Shannon's, Tom prepared a late-night snack of toast, jam, marmalade, peanut butter, cheese, tomatoes, and just about everything else he managed to find in the fridge. There were no burgers, but no one seemed too bothered about it.

He placed the tray on the coffee table and sat on the floor, next to Shannon. 'Don't worry, Shan, we'll find the beast next time.'

Shannon sighed and reached for a slice of toast.

Rhydian and Maddy had made the drinks and were putting them on a tray in the kitchen.

'I can still taste that thistle root,' Maddy whispered.

'I had no choice,' Rhydian said. 'It's the antidote to wolfsbane.'

'Yeah, thanks.'

Rhydian picked up the tray. 'So are you still keen to tell all?'

Maddy shook her head. 'No, not now.' She smiled. 'But I am still hungry.'

Twenty-one

Tom was on edge. The County Cup final was only days away. The good news was that Bradlington High had made it to the final. The not-so-good news was that their opponents were Baron's Mill, the team that had beaten them at the same stage for the past two years.

And there was a further worry. Bradlington's regular goalkeeper was injured and his replacement, Liam Hunter, was nowhere near as good. It wasn't surprising; Liam usually played in midfield.

Liam wasn't a terrible keeper; he just didn't like playing in goal. During a kick around he was half-heartedly facing up to some shots and made little effort to stop a fairly tame effort from team captain, Jimi Chen.

Jimi reacted angrily. 'Liam! You should have got to that, it was easy!'

Liam picked up the ball and angrily booted it away. 'What d'you expect? I'm a midfielder!'

Sam Dodds, who usually had to be content with a seat on the subs bench, had been promoted into Liam's midfield position and was relishing lining up for the final. 'Miss Graham put you in goal, there's nothing we can do about it.'

'Yeah, well, you would say that,' Liam moaned. 'If I was in my proper position you'd be back on the bench, where you belong.'

'Pack it in, you two,' Jimi yelled as he retrieved the ball. 'We've got a match to win on Friday.'

He looked across to Tom, one of Bradlington's star strikers, and sent over a searching pass. Tom took it in his stride and from a long way out, tried an adventurous shot. He hit the ball hard and a little too well and then watched in horror as it shot like a bullet towards the school building and a large window.

'Tom!' Jimi yelled.

'Oh no!' Tom shouted at the same moment.

Rhydian had just emerged from the building with Maddy. He heard the shouts, glanced up and saw the ball hurtling towards the window. Acting on pure, Wolfblood instinct he leapt, and to the amazed stares of footballers and onlookers, got one hand to the ball and knocked it away.

The footballers stared in stunned silence while the onlookers, led by the Three Ks, broke into rapturous applause.

Jimi turned to Sam. 'Sam?'

'Yeah?'

'Go and get Miss Graham.'

* * *

Fifteen minutes later, a slightly bemused Rhydian was on the pitch standing between the goalposts.

Miss Graham, along with Tom, Liam, Sam, most of the other members of the team and a good proportion of Year 9, including Maddy, stood watching and waiting as Jimi lined up a penalty.

'Look,' Rhydian sighed, 'I've told you before, football isn't my thing.'

'Just play along, mate,' Tom called.

'All you have to do is stop the ball going into the goal,' Jimi said.

Jimi was the team's regular penalty taker and he wasn't going to make this easy for Rhydian. He ran up and hit the ball low to Rhydian's right. Rhydian didn't move and the ball crunched into the back of the net.

A groan ran around the crowd and Tom looked away, embarrassed for his friend. It appeared to most onlookers that the wonder save had been a fluke.

'Didn't you hear what I said?' Jimi snapped angrily. 'Stop the ball! Or do you think you're too cool to dive?'

Rhydian sighed and shook his head. 'Do it again.'

'Oh, I don't want to embarrass you!'

'Just do it again.'

'Jimi!' Miss Graham said. 'Take the penalty.'

This time Jimi placed the ball on the spot very

deliberately, with the intention of making Rhydian look a total fool.

He picked his spot; top corner, unstoppable if he hit it right. And he did. The ball flew like an arrow towards the corner of the net. Rhydian leapt to his left and palmed the ball away with a second spectacular save.

Even Jimi gasped. He nodded his reluctant approval. 'What d'you think, miss?' he said to Miss Graham.

'I think,' the teacher replied, 'that we have a new keeper.'

'Yes!' Liam shouted. 'And I'm back in midfield!'

'Oh, miss!' Sam said. It meant that he was back on the bench.

Tom ran over to Rhydian. 'Incredible save, mate.'

Rhydian shrugged. 'Yeah, well, don't expect me to win this match single-handed. I don't get all this fuss about a game anyway.'

'No?' Tom said. He thought for a moment. 'On the field, right, all the things you're not good at . . .' he glanced towards Jimi Chen, '. . . and the people you don't get on with, all that fades away. You're part of something bigger. You're part of a team.'

Rhydian grinned and shook his head. 'Yeah, that really sounds like me, eh?'

Rhydian was walking through the woods, on his way home, or as he thought of it, his latest home. But this time it was different. His foster parents, the Vaughans, were nice enough, but it was Maddy and her parents who made him think that he might just have found a place that could finally be called home.

He was smiling, thinking back to the football and his sudden elevation to potential cup-winning hero. News of his inclusion in the team rapidly spread around the school. Now everyone reckoned they would be at the final, even Shannon, who usually said she saw absolutely no point in groups of people chasing a bit of leather around a field. The Three Ks had announced that they would be cheerleading and had already begun writing their chant and practising their routine.

Rhydian had always been a loner, but gradually he was beginning to think that there was something not entirely unpleasant about being part of something, and part of a team, as had Tom said.

Suddenly he stopped smiling and his Wolfblood senses engaged. Someone, or something, was nearby. Watching him, tracking him.

He stopped walking and he waited, listening, his eyes flicking from one point to another.

A twig snapped, as loud as thunder to Rhydian, and there, standing in his path just five metres ahead was a woman. She had long, dark hair and wild eyes and her clothes were ragged and ancient. Her eyes were locked on Rhydian's.

'What do you want?' Rhydian breathed. 'Who are you?'

The woman's lips moved and formed words in a language that Rhydian couldn't follow.

'What? I don't understand you.'

She spoke again, this time in heavily accented English. 'I'm your mother.'

Rhydian stared; confused, bewildered. 'You can't be . . . I don't have a . . .'

'I am, Rhydian. I am your mother. My name is Ceri.'

Rhydian had dreamed of this moment but now he was filled with dread. He didn't want to believe that the wild, ragged creature staring at him could actually be his mother. But he knew it was true.

'No!' he yelled.

And then he turned and ran.

Twenty-two

Rhydian could not get the vision of his bizarre encounter out of his mind. How could this wild, strange woman claiming to be the mother he'd long forgotten suddenly walk back into his life? What did she want? What did she expect, now, after so long?

He slept badly and drifted through the following day as though he were sleepwalking, unable to focus and unable to concentrate. He couldn't speak to anyone about it, not even Maddy, even though she had sensed something was wrong.

The last training session on the day before the match was fixed for after school. Rhydian went through the motions of changing and pulling on borrowed football boots as though in a dream, as though it was all happening to someone else.

He didn't hear a word as he and the rest of the team gathered around Miss Graham while she spoke about team tactics. All Rhydian heard was a distant voice but the words going round and round in his head were, '*I'm your mother. I'm your mother.*'

'Rhydian! Rhydian, are you listening to me?'

Rhydian was suddenly aware of Miss Graham. 'Sorry, miss, what?'

'I said, get in goal! We're starting!'

'Yeah, sorry.'

Events on the pitch passed him by for a few minutes and fortunately the ball came nowhere near. But then, at a corner kick, with defenders and attackers clustering round, Rhydian took his position on the goal line.

Someone rose for a header and the ball struck Rhydian's shoulder and dropped at Tom's feet. He had the simplest task of tapping it into the net.

'Oh, wake up, Welshie!' Jimi Chen yelled.

'Jimi!' Miss Graham shouted, but she didn't look happy with either the performance or concentration level displayed by the team's new goalkeeper.

The session didn't get any better and by the time the players were back in the changing room the short-lived mood of optimism had totally disappeared. No one said a word to Rhydian while he showered and changed but then Tom came over to offer a few words of encouragement. 'Look, mate,' he said kindly, 'don't worry about it. Match day is always much better.'

Jimi Chen couldn't resist having his say. 'It's always the same with losers; afraid of losing, so they don't try.'

Rhydian scowled. 'Are you saying I'm scared of losing?'

'I'm saying you're not team material.'

'Fine,' Rhydian said. He had a lot more on his mind than football; football was totally unimportant now. Walking out, he threw the borrowed boots to the floor and they slid under a bench.

'Looks like you're back in goal,' Jimi said to Liam.

Rhydian had to speak to Maddy; he could no longer keep his feelings bottled up. He sent her a text and they arranged to meet at Bernie's.

Once there they bought drinks and had hardly settled at a corner table before Rhydian blurted out everything that had happened.

Maddy had been expecting something serious, but nothing like this. 'You *met* her? Where?'

'In the woods, on the way home.'

'But . . . but what's she doing here?'

'I don't know, I ran away, I couldn't . . .' He was suddenly furious. 'She can't just turn up like this. She left me in the middle of nowhere, Maddy; I could have died. What kind of mother does that?'

It was a question that Maddy couldn't possibly answer. 'You don't know why she left you; only she knows that. If you want to know the truth you have to . . .'

The words dried on Maddy's lips. She was looking

over at the open doorway. A woman stood there, staring at them and Maddy knew instantly that this was Rhydian's mother.

Rhydian had his back to the door. He heard soft footsteps as his mother approached but he didn't look up.

'Please?' she said.

Rhydian hesitated. He glanced at Maddy for guidance and she gave the slightest of nods. Still not making eye contact, Rhydian gestured with his head to the empty chair at the table. Maddy picked up the milkshake she'd been nursing and went to the counter, where she sat on one of the stools. She realised she should have allowed Rhydian and his mother their privacy but couldn't stop herself from engaging her Wolfblood hearing. They exchanged a few stilted words but then Rhydian became angry.

'What are you doing here?' he hissed. 'You're on Maddy's territory.'

Maddy could feel the wild Wolfblood's eyes boring into her back as she snarled her reply contemptuously. 'I go where I please. And what will the tame Wolfbloods do about it?'

'What do you *want*?' Rhydian asked.

'*You* don't have to be afraid.'

'I'm not afraid. But I want to know why you're here?'

'I want my beautiful boy.'

'Oh, right,' Rhydian snapped. 'Well, you're twelve years too late.'

'I couldn't help it; I couldn't find you. I'd left you safe while we went hunting and when I came back they were taking you away.'

'You could have gone to social services; you could have told them you were my mum.'

'They'd have locked me up!'

'Not if you'd tried to live like a human being!'

'That's worse than being locked up!'

They stared at each other for long, searching moments.

'Why now?' Rhydian said eventually.

Ceri smiled for the first time. 'I sensed your first transformation. I knew it was time for you to lead the life you were born for.'

Rhydian shook his head but before he could answer he heard Jimi Chen's voice as he came in with Liam and Sam. 'Oh, so this is where Welshie's hiding.'

The newcomers went to the counter, noticing with interest that Maddy was sitting alone while Rhydian was across the room with a strange-looking woman.

His mother glared in their direction. 'Your new friend has made you tame,' she said to Rhydian. 'Like them.'

'You know nothing about me,' Rhydian breathed.

'And Maddy's pack were here for me when you were too busy running wild.'

'Hey, Bernie, has something gone off in here?' Jimi suddenly asked loudly. 'There's a nasty smell about.'

'That's enough,' Bernie snapped. 'Are you three buying anything?'

Rhydian was almost squirming with embarrassment. 'Can we go somewhere else?' he said to Ceri.

'Yes.'

They got up and moved towards the door.

'Oh, it stinks!' Jimi said, as they passed by.

It was an unwise comment to make. Ceri's hand shot out and she grabbed Jimi by an ear. He shrieked in surprise and pain as he was pulled towards the growling, ferocious woman.

'Stop it!' Rhydian yelled.

Rhydian's mother released her hold and with a final snarl she turned and ran from the café, Rhydian following.

They ran to the safety of the woods. Ceri moved through the trees as though she knew every branch and every fallen leaf. She told Rhydian that this woodland and the surrounding moors had been her home for the past few weeks while she waited for the moment to make contact. Rhydian nodded; the attacks on farm animals, the disappearing pets, it all made sense now.

'Back there at the café, they could have called the police,' he said as they walked. 'People know you've been sleeping rough out here.'

'The police wouldn't find me, no one would.'

'You're a Wolfblood, not invisible.'

Ceri shook her head. 'Wolfbloods *are* invisible. We walk in the margins of the world. We are shadow and night and the strength of the moon; we are beyond the understanding of humans.' She stopped and stared into her son's eyes. 'There are senses you've never used, things you can do that your tame friends will never know. We call it Eolas. I can teach you how to use it.'

Rhydian was gradually becoming accustomed to this strange, wild woman. He knew deep down that despite everything there was a bond between them that could never be broken.

They walked and talked and Rhydian lost track of time as Ceri told him Wolfblood mysteries, while he listened intently. It grew dark and the moon rose, not a full moon but enough to bathe the woodland and the moors in soft silver light.

They stopped to rest, and Rhydian leaned back against a rock, gazing up at the moon, thinking through everything Ceri had said.

'So . . . so I should try and do what?'

'Don't *try*. Humans *try*. We listen to our instincts.'

'Listen to my instincts. I . . . I want to but . . . I can't do this.'

'Look at me!' Ceri ordered.

Rhydian turned his head and stared into his mother's eyes. They were dark, deep and hypnotic. Her voice had softened from the angry snarl of earlier and become gentle and persuasive. 'Feel the earth under you, feel the wind over you. Feel the clouds and the sky.'

As Ceri spoke, Rhydian sensed something changing; his world was gradually shifting, travelling to another plane and another place.

'You are part of everything. You *are* nature, you are wild.'

And then he was. Wild. Free. He could see and hear and feel everything. At first it was as though he was looking down on the world, his entire whole world. And then he was moving through it at incredible speed, but still seeing everything. Seeing, sensing, experiencing everything. He saw Maddy, he saw her parents, he saw school, he saw everything.

It was Eolas.

He laughed. 'It's fantastic. I get it, I get it!'

'It's beautiful when you are part of nature,' Ceri told him. 'The pack runs with Eolas, that is how we exist.'

'And . . . you want me to go with you?'

'Yes.'

'Forever?'

'What have you got here?'

'I've got friends,' Rhydian said slowly.

Ceri looked at him closely. 'Rhydian, if you come with me you'll have a pack. A family.'

Twenty-three

Rhydian thought about it all that night and by morning had made up his mind. He was going. Back to nature, back to the wild, with his mother, with his pack. He was going to live as a wild Wolfblood.

There was no way he could explain his decision to his friends, not even to Maddy. Not even she could understand everything; she had never experienced Eolas. But Rhydian couldn't just leave; he had to say goodbye. There was time at least for that.

School was buzzing at the prospect of the County Cup final that evening. Rhydian arrived late and as the day slipped quickly by he found no opportunity to break his life-changing news to Maddy.

Towards the end of the day he was standing by his locker as Maddy approached him and spotted the sleeping bag and rucksack stuffed with a few clothes that he had stashed there earlier.

'What are you doing?' Maddy asked anxiously.

Rhydian took a deep breath; this was it. 'I'm going with her.'

Maddy was too stunned to reply.

'She's my mum. She can teach me things.'

'But . . . but you can't just run away.'

'It won't be the first time but . . . well, it will be the first time I'll be sad to leave people behind.'

Maddy was desperate. 'I won't let you. I'll tell Jeffries and I'll ring your parents.'

'You won't, Maddy,' Rhydian said gently. 'Tom or Shannon would, they'd think they were doing the right thing. But you know the truth, I'm going to live the life I was born for.'

'But what if it's not? What if you go with her and you hate it?'

Rhydian shook his head. 'You have to let me try, Maddy.'

He closed the locker door and walked away, leaving Maddy near to tears. She knew there was nothing she could do to make him change his mind.

The countdown to kick-off had begun. The Baron's Mill team and their travelling band of supporters had arrived, and Rhydian lingered by the changing room waiting for a chance to speak to Tom. 'I owe you an apology,' he said the moment Tom appeared. 'The football team, all that stuff. I let you down.'

Tom rarely bore grudges. 'Nah, I was stupid, thinking you'd be brilliant when you don't even like football.'

'But how can I make it up to you? I want to leave with a clean slate.'

'Leave? What you on about?'

Rhydian realised he was in danger of saying too much. 'I mean, leave *it*, the issue. I don't want any bad feelings.'

'There's no bad feelings. But if you really want to put it right you can join the team again.'

'But I can't.'

'Why not?'

'I . . . I don't belong.'

Tom shook his head. 'Mate, you belong where you want to be. If you want to be in the team, just for one game, then make it happen.'

'But . . . but can I do that? Just for one game?'

Tom smiled. 'It's our biggest game of the season. We want to win it.'

When the Bradlington team ran on to the pitch with Rhydian bringing up the rear in the goalkeeper's jersey there were many surprised and delighted faces among the crowd.

With the backing of all but one of the team, Miss Graham had allowed Rhydian to return to the starting line-up. Liam was overjoyed to be once again in midfield and Jimi had personally retrieved the football boots from under the bench where they had remained since Rhydian stormed out the previous day. Only Sam was disappointed – he was back on the bench.

Maddy was official match photographer. She was standing on the touchline alongside Shannon, who knew absolutely nothing about football but had promised to do her best to make sense of what she was about to observe on the pitch.

There was a huge crowd, with great support from both schools. And once the match was underway, the head of Year 9, Mr Jeffries, urged on the Bradlington team as loudly as anyone, while the Three Ks kept most spectators amused and entertained with their cheerleading routines.

It was a tense and closely fought game. Tom came close to scoring a couple of times and Rhydian made one or two decent if unspectacular saves but by half-time there was no score. Midway through the second period Liam was substituted and Sam took his place in midfield.

Maddy took plenty of action photos but all the while she was thinking that the nearer the match came to ending the closer they were to Rhydian leaving forever. She tried to force it to the back of her mind and concentrate on her photographs, but it was impossible.

The clock ticked down with more half-chances and near-misses, but with the match virtually over there was still no score.

Maddy checked her watch. 'That's it; the ninety minutes are up.'

Shannon looked confused. 'So why are they still playing?'

'Injury time.'

'Oh. Are we winning?'

'Shannon! It's nil–nil; have you even been watching?'

Before Shannon could reply there was a shrill blast from the referee's whistle, but not for the end of the match. Sam, trying hard to impress, had been a little too reckless with a tackle, bringing down an opponent as he closed on the goal. It was a clear penalty with only seconds remaining and the Baron's Mill supporters were already celebrating.

'Oh no, penalty,' Maddy said.

'Is that good?'

'No! If they score it's all over for us.'

The Baron's Mill captain placed the ball on the penalty spot and took four long steps back. There were a few shouts of 'Come on, Rhydian,' from the Bradlington supporters and then the crowd went silent.

Rhydian stood on the goal line, his Wolfblood senses activated, totally focused on making the save.

Every other player on the pitch, apart from the Baron's Mill goalkeeper, was on the edge of the box, waiting for the penalty to be taken.

The Baron's Mill captain ran up and struck the ball

perfectly, it looked a certain goal. Rhydian leapt like a wolf and not only saved the ball, but caught it cleanly in both hands. It was an amazing save.

As a mixture of cheers and groans echoed around the pitch, Rhydian spotted Tom running towards the Baron's Mill goal and calling for the ball. He was still in his own half but it would take an incredibly long and accurate throw from Rhydian to reach him. The ball soared skywards, over the heads of the Bradlington and Baron's Mill players and dropped perfectly at Tom's feet. With defenders chasing frantically after him he crossed the halfway line with only the opposing goalkeeper to beat.

It was not an easy chance, but Tom was ice-cool on the football pitch. As the goalkeeper came out and a chasing defender tried a desperate lunging tackle, Tom feinted one way and then the other and then slotted the ball firmly into the net.

As he leapt into the air, screaming in delight, the referee's whistle sounded for the end of the match.

Bradlington had won the cup.

Rhydian sat in the changing room reliving the magical moments that had followed the final whistle. His team-mates had hoisted him on to their shoulders and carried him from the pitch to the echo of joyous cheers before they were presented with the trophy and their medals.

It was a triumph, a team triumph, although Rhydian and Tom were hailed as the match-winning heroes. They lined up for team photographs and Maddy made sure she got a special shot of the two of them together, grinning happily as they held the trophy.

Back in the changing room the celebrations continued with every moment of the match discussed and debated.

'Burgers at Bernie's,' Jimi said to Rhydian as he went to leave with Liam and Sam. 'You coming?'

'Maybe later.'

Jimi nodded. 'Great save. And great throw.'

Rhydian smiled. 'Thanks, Jimi.'

Finally only Rhydian and Tom remained. Tom finished packing his kit and strode to the door. 'I'll see you in a bit, yeah?'

Rhydian didn't answer. He just smiled at his friend and teammate. A few minutes later he walked from the changing room, deep in thought. Maddy was waiting nearby, as he had hoped she would be.

'Hey,' she said, trying to look cheerful and happy, 'it's the man of the match.'

'Tom scored the goal,' Rhydian said. 'I've never seen him so happy.'

'I've never seen *you* that happy,' Maddy replied. 'Not in human form, anyway.'

'It was great; winning, being part of the team.'

'Belonging?'

'Yeah, I guess.'

'It's not too late to change your mind.'

Twenty metres ahead someone stepped from behind the building. It was Ceri.

'Or is this where I say goodbye?' Maddy said, struggling to hold back her tears.

'It's . . . it's my choice, Maddy.'

'I hate goodbyes, anyway.' Maddy was determined that Rhydian would not see her cry. She hurried away and did not look back.

Rhydian felt more torn than ever. He wanted to call out to Maddy but Ceri was waiting impatiently. 'We should be gone by now!' she said when Rhydian joined her.

'I told you I'd see you when I'd finished.'

'Finished what?'

'Football. Did you watch?'

Ceri sneered. 'I don't watch humans playing their games.'

'Well, you should have,' Rhydian snapped. His mind was in turmoil, still filled with thoughts of the match and of Tom and the others, and most of all, of Maddy. 'Then you might have understood why . . . why . . . why I'm not coming with you.'

'What?' his mother said completely shocked. 'You want to stay here?'

'You should have watched me. I was part of something. Something I was good at, not something I was born into. It was my choice, my *real* choice.'

'But I'm offering you freedom! The Wolfblood life!'

'You could stay around. Be here, be part of my life.'

Ceri's anger was building. 'Did *she* do this? Your tame wolf friend?'

'Don't you *ever* call Maddy tame!'

His mother snarled furiously and lowered her head, her eyes blazing and her hands forming into claws. For a moment, Rhydian thought she was taking wolf form to attack him. But he stood his ground, defying her, daring her to strike.

'She's corrupted you,' Ceri yelled. 'I'm your mother!'

'The mother who wasn't there for me!"

Rhydian's furious words were more than Ceri could take. With an anguished snarl, she turned and ran. Rhydian watched her go, staring until long after she had disappeared, wondering if this was the last he would ever see of his mother.

Then he heard footsteps.

It was Tom. 'Thought I'd come back for our man of the match. Shannon said she'd meet us at Bernie's.'

Rhydian smiled. 'Cool.' He felt a rush of happiness knowing he had made the right decision. They walked across the playground heading for the school exit and chatting through, yet again, the final moments of the match.

Maddy was not far away. She was waiting for a bus but in no hurry to get home and explain to her parents how Rhydian had gone for good. Suddenly she raised her head and sniffed the air. 'Rhydian!'

She ran down the road and came face to face with them as they turned the corner.

'We're going to Bernie's,' Rhydian said before she had a chance to speak. 'You coming?'

Maddy nodded, unable to say how deliriously happy she felt at that moment. So she squeezed between them and linked her arms through theirs. 'Bernie's,' she said joyfully.

Twenty-four

The night of the full moon was with them again. It meant an anxious day for Maddy's parents after a promise from Maddy and Rhydian that they would spend the night in the safety of the den, rather than run wild again as wolves.

Rhydian was not happy but had eventually agreed to it. It would be his first time locked in the den, and Maddy's too. Their previous transformations had led to big trouble for them both, so Emma and Daniel were relieved and delighted when their daughter and Rhydian arrived after school.

They went through to the living room while Maddy's parents finished preparing dinner. Rhydian slumped on the sofa but Maddy was on edge and started pacing nervously up and down.

Rhydian spoke quietly. 'We don't have to do this, you know. I don't care how your mum and dad justify it; it's still a cage. And it's unnatural.'

Maddy stopped pacing. 'We promised and we can't let them down again. And you said you were OK with it.'

'That was when full moon was a long way away. Now even this room feels about half its normal size.'

'Yeah, I know what you mean. But I won't go against Mam and Dad.'

The tension was getting to Rhydian too. He got up, went to the window and stared out at the darkening sky. 'So for the rest of our lives we have to be locked up on the one night we should be running free.'

'Yes! No! Oh, that's not fair!' Maddy snapped. 'I don't know, but I can't think about the rest of my life right now.'

'OK,' Rhydian said with an unconvincing shrug of his shoulders. 'We'll do whatever you decide.'

He was heading back to the sofa when Maddy's dad came through from the kitchen. 'Come and have a look at the modifications I made to the security of the den.'

Rhydian and Maddy exchanged a look. The thought of being locked in while the full moon was high was already bad enough, but the idea of seeing the extra security to keep them there made the prospect of it even worse. But they obediently followed Daniel down the stone staircase to the cellar room he had converted into the den.

Before her first transformation it had been Maddy's job to fix the locks that kept her parents secured until daylight, when she would release them. But now that she too was a fully-fledged Wolfblood they had to do the job themselves. And they had to ensure there was no way they could set themselves free when the pull of the moon was at its strongest. So Daniel had put new bolts on the shutters from the coal chute, which meant they could only be opened from the outside. And there were further security improvements too. He slid home the new locking bolt on the barred entrance door to the den. 'Once we're inside no one can get in and we can't get out.' He laughed. 'Not until our paws have changed back to fingers, that is.'

'Great,' Rhydian said, trying to sound enthusiastic. 'You've done a great job, it's very . . . secure.'

He looked at Maddy and raised his eyebrows.

Tom and Shannon were at Bernie's, doing their best to ignore the Three Ks, who were chatting noisily at another table, when the door swung open and a young man in designer sunglasses appeared.

He stood, posing, in the doorway, before removing his sunglasses. His eyes slowly scanned the room as the Three Ks gazed with serious interest. The stranger was tall and handsome and dressed for the outdoors in rugged but fashionable clothes.

'Is Shannon Kelly here?' he asked.

The Ks' faces fell and Shannon timidly raised a hand. Tall, dark strangers didn't usually appear and ask for her, but this one strode over, took her raised hand in his and shook it warmly.

'Kyle Weathers,' he announced. 'I've come a long way to meet you.'

'Er . . . thanks,' Shannon mumbled. 'This is Tom.'

'Tom,' the newcomer said. 'Good to meet you.' He slid into an empty chair and gave Shannon his full attention. 'We're short on daylight, so I'll come straight to the point; the beast is in my sights and you're the girl to help me find it.'

The Three Ks were straining to hear every word while Shannon looked totally bewildered. 'Excuse me?'

'I've been checking out your website and monitoring your blog for the past six months. Your findings are pretty compelling.'

'Oh,' Shannon said, delighted at the compliment. 'So why didn't you leave any comments?'

'Simply because I didn't want to open myself up to replies from fools with no brains and even less imagination.'

Shannon smiled and stared deliberately at the Ks. 'I know exactly what you mean.'

'Now, Shannon,' Kyle said, 'I'm searching the woods tonight and I need an expert. What do you say?'

'But . . . who are you exactly?'

Kyle leaned closer and spoke slowly and sincerely. 'I am you!'

'What?' Shannon said as Tom looked away and rolled his eyes.

'Twelve years ago *I* was the kid who no one believed,' Kyle continued dramatically. 'I saw something, an animal, a creature, I don't know. But I saw it and for a while I tried to convince others that I'd seen something strange, something different.' He sighed and shook his head. 'I don't need to tell you how that went.'

'You certainly do not!'

'There are more things out there than you and I know about, Shannon, so I . . . I photograph and study these things.'

'I see,' Shannon murmured, enthralled, and delighted at last to come face to face with another believer.

'So, Shannon, if you will do me the honour of being my guide, tonight, I will find the beast for you.'

Shannon gave the Three Ks a long satisfied grin before turning her smile on Kyle. 'I'd be delighted,' she said loudly. 'And Tom will come too.'

'Oh, will I?' Tom said.

Kyle was not travelling alone. Parked outside Bernie's stood a truck with a covered rear section. At the wheel sat another man, who Kyle introduced as his assistant, Steve. He was listening to music through earphones and when Shannon and Tom said hello he just nodded but said nothing.

'Steve's a man of few words,' Kyle told them. 'Loves his music.'

Parked immediately behind the truck was a small car. A girl, who Tom guessed was probably about eighteen, was inside. Next to her on the front passenger seat was a video camera. Kyle introduced the third member of his team as Jo and then went back to the truck to confer with Steve.

'So, you're with Kyle?' Tom asked Jo, trying to look and sound cool.

'I'm *filming* Kyle. There's a difference.'

'Oh, right. So you're a film student, are you?'

'Very observant,' Jo told him, obviously unimpressed at his attempts to get to know her. 'And I'd like to concentrate on filming, if you don't mind.'

Tom rolled his eyes and nodded. 'Right.'

They were almost ready to go down into the cellar to lock themselves in for the night. Daniel was making his way around the house, ensuring that all the windows and doors were secured, while Emma finished up in the kitchen.

Maddy and Rhydian sat at the kitchen table, both feeling as anxious as they looked. And Emma sensed it. 'What's going on, you two?'

'Nothing,' Maddy said quickly. 'Just not looking forward to tonight.'

'Well, it's the way it has to be.'

'But when we were out before on full moon . . .'

'It's never happening again, Maddy. It's not safe out there for Wolfbloods.'

Daniel came through from the living room. 'All it takes is one person to spot us and they'll hunt us down. That's what they do.'

'Now, come on,' Emma said. 'It's time for us to go down.'

Maddy sighed and got up from her chair.

'Our first time as a family,' Daniel said, leading the way down the stairs. 'I feel like I should make a speech.'

Emma was following. 'You'd better make it quick if you don't want to end up growling.'

They began to sort out the food and water that would sustain them through the long night when Emma looked up and noticed Maddy still in the doorway. Rhydian stood behind her.

'Come on, both of you,' Emma said, 'the moon won't wait.'

But Maddy could not take the final step inside. 'I'm sorry, Mam,' she said, pulling the barred door shut and pushing home the locking bolt. Before either parent could react, Maddy had slammed the outer door shut and turned the first key in the lock, just as she always had.

'Maddy!' her mother screamed from inside the den. 'Maddy, open this door!'

The second two locks clicked into place. Emma and Daniel were trapped in the den until someone set them free.

'Maddy!' Emma yelled again. 'Maddy!'

Twenty-five

Shannon and Tom were with Kyle and his team at a spot deep in the woods. The full moon pierced the tree canopy, casting eerie shadows, as Steve sorted gear in the back of the truck and Jo checked her camera.

'Farm animals and pets have been going missing for weeks,' Shannon told Kyle. 'It has to be the beast; I tracked it to this area before.'

Kyle was impressed. He stalked the wide clearing, praising Shannon constantly for her good work and telling her that he was convinced the full moon meant they would find the beast that night.

On the far side of the clearing, Tom was still trying to establish friendly relations with Jo. 'Anything I can do to help?'

Jo pointed across the clearing. 'See that tree over there?'

'Yeah?'

'Go and stand under it and leave me alone.'

But instead of slinking away Tom just laughed. 'Good one.'

Jo glanced up from her camera and smiled at Tom

for the first time. 'Yeah, all right. You can look after my camera bag, but don't break anything!'

Tom grinned. 'Promise.' He picked up the bag and slung it over one shoulder. 'So what's the deal with you and Kyle?'

'He needed someone to put his work on camera and I need a great graduation film to kick-start my career. Now, before I tell you my entire life story, we need to make a start.'

She went quickly into action, taking footage of Kyle and Shannon and getting them to say a few words of introduction. Shannon spoke a little shyly, but Kyle was as confident on camera as off, and highly dramatic. His closing comment made the watching Tom cringe. 'The full moon has risen and the creatures of the night are coming out to play!'

'Yeah, we'll see,' Tom muttered as Jo stopped filming.

At the rear of the truck Steve, who had still not uttered a word but had at least removed his earphones, was pulling a tarpaulin off a large, square object.

'What's that?' Shannon asked, hurrying over for a closer view.

'Just a secure container,' Kyle told her. 'It's harmless but inescapable.'

Shannon looked horrified. 'But . . .'

Kyle smiled another of his winning smiles. 'Yes, Shannon, we're going to *catch* the beast.'

'But I didn't bring you here to catch it!'

'Shannon, relax. This is merely for our safety. The beast could turn on us; we have to be careful. And don't worry, I'm not in the business of caging wild animals. We'll put it in the container to take a look, that's all.'

'Right,' Shannon said, trying to keep calm. 'It just . . . well, suddenly, it all just got real.'

'It is real, Shannon, and we're going to show the world it's real.'

Tom was not so convinced. 'But what makes you so sure you'll find the beast tonight?'

'Firstly this,' Kyle answered, going to the back of the truck and taking out an aerosol canister. 'In this, Tom, is bait, a scientifically engineered aroma that is totally irresistible – if you happen to be a beast.' He pulled out another item, this time from a cool box. It was a large joint of raw meat, still on the bone. 'And here we have your basic Sunday roast.' He aimed the canister and sprayed the meat. 'Add the two together and we create food heaven for our beast.'

Intrigued but slightly uneasy, Shannon and Tom watched as Kyle strode to the centre of the clearing to rest the joint on the ground. The pungent smell of raw flesh was unmistakeable.

'Back to the safety of the truck, everyone,' Kyle ordered. 'And now we wait, and somehow I don't think we'll be waiting for long.'

He was right. Maddy and Rhydian had transformed swiftly in the moonlight before loping away from the farmhouse to their natural habitat, the woodland. They played like puppies at first, running and frolicking among the leaves, but soon they were hungry.

The scientifically created aroma combined with the raw meat wafted through the woodland, and quickly captured the total attention of the two young wolves. Moving together, they slunk noiselessly through the night, stalking their prey.

Shannon, Tom, Kyle and Jo were crouched low, close to the truck. Steve hovered nearby.

Suddenly Jo spoke in little more than a whisper as she focused her camera. 'I see movement: ten o'clock.'

All eyes turned to the spot and everyone glimpsed stealthy movement as something approached through the bushes and trees. Jo was right; the beast was coming.

Kyle reached into a bag at his side and brought out a rifle.

Shannon's eyes widened. 'What are you doing?'

'Ssshh! It's a tranquilliser gun. Perfectly harmless, vets use them all the time. It'll put it out for a few minutes. Don't miss this, Jo.'

'I never miss,' Jo said as she filmed. 'Make sure you don't.'

Kyle peered down the sights, pulled the trigger and

immediately reached into a pocket to take out another tranquilliser dart.

'Did you miss?' Tom breathed.

'No, there are two of them.'

'Two!' Shannon said, complete baffled.

A wolf howl shattered the silence as Kyle fired again. 'Got 'em.'

'You can come and take a look now,' Kyle called to Shannon and Tom.

He had refused to let them approach until the animals were safely in the containers, just in case they were only stunned and dangerous.

Shannon took the torch that Kyle was holding and shone it into the container. The beam settled on two sleeping animals.

'They're . . . they're wolves!'

'Wolves,' Tom echoed. 'But wolves have been extinct in Britain for years.'

Shannon shook her head in disbelief. 'Everyone thought they'd died out. Maybe they've been here all the time.'

The wolves were already beginning to stir. 'They're waking up,' Shannon said quickly to Kyle. 'You should let them go now.'

Kyle laughed. 'And why would I do that?'

As the mystified Shannon and Tom looked on Kyle

and Steve hauled the container over to the truck and lifted it on to the open back.

'What's going on?' Tom said.

'We'll, I'm not leaving them here for someone else to find. I'll keep them for now, then maybe sell them to a zoo.'

The thought of the animals being caged made Shannon furious. 'No! Let them go! There are enough wolves in zoos!'

'Ah, but not like these wolves. These are special, plucky survivors. There could be a movie in it; I might even be the star.'

'That's all you're interested in,' Tom said angrily. 'You!'

Kyle grinned. 'Er . . . yeah!' He laughed. 'And thanks for your help, kids, but it's way past your bedtime. Say goodbye to the puppies, they're off to their new home. And I'll see you later, Jo.'

Shannon peered through the slats in the container and glimpsed four golden eyes staring balefully out at her, as though the wolves were pleading to be set free. Then Steve threw a tarpaulin over the container and they were completely lost from sight. They began to howl.

Tom turned his anger on Jo. 'You knew about this?'

Jo looked slightly uneasy. 'Well, not exactly. Look, all I wanted to do was get the best possible film.'

'So you let him use us?'

'No!'

The truck pulled away and the wolves continued to howl.

'You've got to help us stop this, Jo!' Tom said, seeing Shannon's distraught face.

'But filmmakers observe, they don't interfere. And Kyle's the bad guy in this, not me.'

'No,' Tom said, shaking his head in disgust, 'you're just scared that if you do help us stop him you won't get a film out of it.'

Jo shrugged of her shoulders. 'Maybe. That's the real world, Tom.'

'But it's not right!'

'I've got it!' Shannon yelled excitedly. She turned to Jo, her eyes blazing. 'We'll give you a better film, much better, with a surprise ending, a twist in the tale. Isn't that what you filmmakers really want?'

Jo raised her eyebrows. 'Keep talking.'

Jo's car bumped along a narrow track. Shannon had explored the woods so often in her search for the beast she was certain it was the shortcut they needed.

And as Jo wrestled with the steering wheel and the car lurched from side to side, Tom was getting an opportunity to try out as film cameraman. With the headlights picking out the way ahead he was filming through the windscreen.

'Now point the camera at Shannon,' Jo instructed, as the car finally moved on to a smoother section of track. 'Tell us why we're in the middle of a chase scene, Shannon?'

Shannon looked directly into the lens and spoke with much more confidence than the first time around. 'We're doing this because Kyle Weathers is a glory hunter who doesn't care what he destroys to get that glory. He's caged two beautiful wolves just to make himself look good and to make money, and we're not going to let him do that!'

'And . . . *cut* . . .' Jo said to Tom.

Tom stopped filming and nodded. 'I could get used to this.'

They made it with only seconds to spare. Bumping on to the main track, Jo brought the car to a skidding halt just as Kyle's truck, with Steve at the wheel, rounded a sweeping bend and was forced to stop.

Shannon leapt out and Jo took the camera from Tom, who ran into the cover of the trees.

Kyle came angrily stomping up to Shannon, who bravely stood her ground. 'Get out of my way.'

'You said you were just like me,' Shannon said. 'You said you *were* me.'

Kyle's winning smile and charming ways had completely disappeared. 'Yeah, well, no one's that weird.'

'And we're not moving until you let the wolves go.'

Jo was filming the tense stand-off but Kyle didn't seem to care. 'Just go home. You're out of your depth with this.'

'So, everything you said was a lie?' Shannon said, not budging an inch.

'Finally, you get it.'

'I trusted you, but I should have known you were too good to be true.'

'Yeah, I guess you should.'

'But I'm glad I'm not like you.'

Kyle shook his head. 'Look, if your plan was to appeal to my better nature, it's not going to work; I don't have one.'

Shannon waited for a moment and then glanced towards the camera before looking back at Kyle. She smiled. 'That was Plan A, Kyle. Plan B was to keep you talking while Tom went to the back of your truck and let the wolves go.'

Kyle stared as though he couldn't believe what he was hearing. Then he spun around and ran to the rear of the truck. Tom was standing there smiling. The container was open and the wolves had gone.

'Steve!' Kyle yelled. 'Steve!'

He rushed to the driver's door and pulled it open. Steve sat with a contented smile on his face, listening to music through his earphones and oblivious to everything that had gone on around him.

Slamming the door, Kyle turned angrily on Shannon and Tom as Jo continued to film. 'You've slowed me down, that's all,' he snarled. 'But I've still got the bait and I'll be back for your wolves!'

He climbed into the truck and they heard him barking out orders to Steve. The engine coughed into life, and as they watched the vehicle slowly and carefully manoeuvred around Jo's car. Finally the truck disappeared down the track.

'Lucky he didn't try that first,' Shannon said. 'He's right about the bait, though.'

'What, this bait, you mean?' Tom said, removing the canister from inside his jacket. He grinned and turned to Jo. 'I think I'm ready for my close-up now.'

Twenty-six

Maddy and Rhydian had had an incredibly narrow escape. They'd pushed their luck to the absolute limit and knew they were unlikely to be so lucky again. Not that there was much prospect of further full moon freedom any time in the near future.

Emma and Daniel were fuming when their daughter released them from the den soon after daylight. Despite Rhydian's offer to say it had been his idea, Maddy insisted on taking all the blame. It didn't help, especially when she confessed that they had actually been captured and caged, and that only Shannon's quick thinking had saved them.

The mood was icy in the Smith household and it looked as though it would remain that way for some time, certainly until after the next full moon. And at least until after the next full moon, Maddy was grounded.

At school, Tom and Shannon almost exploded with excitement when they told Maddy and Rhydian about the events in the woods, and how they had foiled Kyle's plan to keep the two beautiful wolves.

Maddy and Rhydian could only listen and react as

though they knew nothing about it; but every word they heard only increased their unspoken gratitude to their friends.

They decided to give them both a gift, as they could never tell them exactly how grateful they were. So Rhydian did pencil drawings of two wolves and Maddy framed them in her dad's workshop.

'Wow!' Tom said when he was presented with his drawing. 'That is brilliant.'

'They're amazing,' Shannon added, gazing at hers. 'And they look exactly like the wolves we saw.'

'Oh . . . really?' Rhydian said. He hadn't intended the drawings to be portraits of himself and Maddy in wolf form. 'I . . . I just copied them from photos.'

'Anyway,' Maddy added hurriedly, 'it's a sort of thank you on behalf of the wolves you so bravely rescued.'

Shannon nodded. 'But that was only half the battle. We have to do more to protect them, so I'm going to contact the Department for the Environment.'

'What?' Maddy and Rhydian said together.

'The wolves are in danger; from people like Kyle or farmers with guns. I'm going to get our wolves officially protected.'

'But . . .'

'I saw the way the wolves looked at me, Maddy. They trusted me and I won't let them down.'

'Yeah, but we don't even have proof the wolves even exist,' Tom said.

'But I know how we can get it.'

'How?'

'Kyle's wolf bait. It's irresistible, remember?'

'But I threw the canister away in the woods.'

'Tom, don't be difficult. We'll find it, then attract the wolves and take all the photos we need.' She looked at her three friends one by one. 'We'll meet at Bernie's later. And it's important, so don't let me down. Or the wolves.'

They had to come up with a counter-plan and they had to move quickly. Both Maddy and Rhydian realised that if they were exposed to the wolf bait it would almost certainly lead to them transforming. Their only options were to avoid going on the mercy mission or get to the canister first to dispose of it.

Letting Shannon down again was out of the question, so the decision was made; they would find the canister and get rid of it for good. But even that was risky if the canister was damaged and leaking.

Maddy had an idea. 'Dad's got some filter masks in his workshop; I'll go get us some. Meet me in the woods.'

There was no time to lose and no time for further

discussion. Once Maddy got home she went straight to the workshop and had just found the masks when her dad walked in. 'Taking up woodwork, are you?'

'Dad, I don't have time to explain now.'

'Try.'

'I'm trying to stop a big problem.'

Daniel frowned. 'What, again, Maddy? And I suppose it involves Rhydian?'

'It involves us all. Look, Shannon wants to get the wolves protected by law. So she thinks if she finds that chemical bait she can release it to attract the wolves and –'

'And then take photos for the authorities,' Daniel said, interrupting.

Maddy nodded. 'Me and Rhydian are going to find the canister so we can get rid of it.'

'Oh no, Maddy,' Daniel said, shaking his head, 'you're going nowhere. You're grounded, remember!'

The scent was familiar but it wasn't Maddy's scent. Rhydian was waiting at their arranged meeting place on the edge of the woods, and Maddy was late. Rhydian was tempted to call her, but he was not exactly her parent's favourite Wolfblood right now, so he decided to wait for a little longer.

And then the scent was suddenly strong in his

nostrils – a Wolfblood scent. He looked around, his senses fully tuned in. The woodland was still, nothing appeared to be moving, but the scent grew stronger all the while.

Rhydian moved on, slowly and carefully at first, but when he increased his pace he heard something step lightly on the woodland floor. He turned around; there was nothing to be seen. He walked on again and then broke into a run and heard rustling in the covering bushes. Certain now that he was being pursued, he stopped dead and spun around. Again he saw nothing and there was no sound except for distant birdsong. But the scent was even stronger. This time Rhydian ran quickly, using Wolfblood speed, and after thirty metres he leapt almost noiselessly into the lower branches of a tree.

The boy appeared moments later. Long-haired and dirty-faced, his scruffy clothes instantly reminded Rhydian of the way his mother, Ceri, dressed. He looked about twelve, but it was difficult to be certain. Rhydian waited as the boy approached stealthily and then stopped walking.

The boy knew he was being watched and he knew exactly where Rhydian was. He looked up. 'So they haven't made you completely human, then?'

'Who are you?' Rhydian asked. 'You smell like . . .'

'Like you?'

Rhydian did not reply.

'I'm Bryn. Your brother. And I've come to take you home.'

Twenty-seven

The argument between Maddy and her dad was still raging when Maddy's phone began to ring. She fetched it guiltily from a pocket, pretty certain who was calling.

'Rhydian?' her dad asked.

Maddy nodded and answered the call. 'Yes?'

Rhydian came straight to the point. 'I've got a brother, a little brother, and he's here.'

'What?'

'What's he done now?' Daniel said.

'Is Ceri there too?' Maddy said into the phone.

'No!'

'Ceri?' Daniel said. 'What's going on, Maddy?'

'Rhydian's little brother's showed up,' Maddy told him.

'Oh, wonderful! Another one!'

'Maddy?' Rhydian said. 'Maddy, are you there?'

'Yes!'

'Why didn't she tell me I had a brother?'

'I don't know, maybe she thought one shock at a time was enough!'

'He says he wants to take me home! What do I do, Maddy?'

'I don't know, Rhydian! Stay with him; try to work it out. Look, I have to go, I've got problems here too.'

As Maddy ended the call she saw her mum in the doorway. 'You certainly have, young lady.'

Emma had heard more than enough. 'All these years we've told you to hide the truth, Maddy; it wasn't to spoil your fun. There are people out there who would hurt Wolfbloods if they could.'

'I know that, and I've kept our secret.'

'Just! And no thanks to Rhydian. We've tried to help him, Maddy. We brought him into our pack, we showed him how to stay safe.'

'And where's that got us?' Daniel said. 'It's been one thing after another. Look, we've talked about this between ourselves for a while now and . . .'

'Talked about what, Dad?'

Emma spoke before Daniel could answer. 'Rhydian. We're finished with him; he's no longer our concern.'

'But you can't . . .'

'I'll lock all the doors and windows,' Daniel said. 'We'll stay in here until Shannon has used up all this wolf bait.'

Maddy could hardly believe what she was hearing. 'But Rhydian's out there, with his brother!'

'And he's out of control, Maddy. And sooner or later he'll get caught and we're not having you going down with him.'

'No!' Maddy yelled. 'I won't let you abandon him!'

'It's not your choice any more,' her mother said coldly. 'Now get up to your room! And stay there!'

Rhydian was quickly discovering that his wild Wolfblood brother truly was wild. with virtually no idea of the ways of the human world.

Gradually and haltingly, the boy admitted that he had not come to find Rhydian with their mother's blessing. He told his brother he'd run away while Ceri was sleeping and was certain that she would be tracking him by now.

'But why did you have to find me?' Rhydian asked him.

'Because she's not the same since she came back without you. She doesn't hunt, she hardly notices me. You're the only thing she thinks about.' He turned his big dark eyes on his brother. 'And I want my mum back.'

Rhydian had to think fast. He couldn't be spotted in the open with this wild-looking boy and face the inevitable questions that would follow, so he decided to take Bryn back to his foster parents' place. They were out, which meant the brothers could wait in safety until Rhydian came up with what to do next.

Bryn stared in awe when they went into the house. It was clear to Rhydian that despite the brave words his little brother was actually scared in the unfamiliar human world. He flinched when Rhydian switched on the kitchen light and then managed to bump into almost everything he encountered, sending a fruit bowl filled with apples and oranges crashing to the kitchen floor. Stepping between the fragments of broken china, he snatched up an apple and hungrily bit into it.

It wasn't exactly to his taste. 'Haven't you got any meat?' he asked through a mouthful of half-chewed apple.

Rhydian shrugged. 'I could cook you a burger?'

'Can't we just hunt?'

'I don't hunt,' Rhydian said. 'Well, not when I'm like this.'

'In the *human* world.'

'Yeah, that's right.' He watched his brother devour the entire apple. 'So tell me, are there any more brothers and sisters I should know about?'

'No.'

'What about a dad?'

Bryn shook his long, shaggy hair. 'Fathers come and go. Mothers stay; mothers take care of you.'

'Yeah? Well, not me.'

'But all she ever talks about is you, her child stolen by humans. That's why you have to come with me.'

The click of a key turning in the front door sounded from the hall. Rhydian's foster parents were back. He glanced at the mess covering the kitchen floor and at his wild-eyed brother and decided that a quick exit was urgently required. 'Come on,' he said quietly and they hurried out through the back door.

Rhydian wasn't quite sure where they would go next. Returning to the woods was not a good idea, especially with the wolf bait canister lying somewhere out there. So they walked towards Stoneybridge and, all the while, Bryn repeated again and again that Rhydian had to return with him to their mother to live the life he was meant to live.

'Look,' Rhydian told him as they neared Bernie's, 'I just can't leave everything here to be with you, and I don't want to.'

Bryn's eyes narrowed. 'Then I'll make you leave.'

'Oh, and how will you do that?'

'By telling the humans who you really are!'

Before Rhydian could stop him Bryn was hurtling towards Bernie's. He burst through the door and skidded to a standstill. 'Does anyone here know my brother?'

The Three Ks were at one table; Jimi, Liam and Sam were at another. Bernie was behind the counter. And everyone was staring in confusion at the wild-eyed, ragged little boy.

'His name's Rhydian!'

'Rhydian!' several voices said together.

'He's a Wolfblood!'

Katrina looked towards her friends for an explanation. 'A what?'

Rhydian came hurrying through the still-open door and immediately knew Bryn had been true to his words.

Kay was first to speak. 'Is he your brother?'

'What's a Wolfblood?' Katrina chimed in.

'Is that a name?' Liam asked. 'Like, Rhydian Wolfblood?'

'He's . . . he's a new foster placement,' Rhydian mumbled. 'He's winding you up, that's all. Come on, Bryn, time to go.'

But Bryn was not moving. 'No, I'm his real brother. Rhydian's not like you, he belongs in the wilderness. We're Wolfbloods. He changes at the full moon. He's a wolf!'

The confused looks vanished and suddenly everyone was roaring with laughter, pointing at Bryn as though he were some sort of comedy act.

'It's true, I tell you, it's true!'

'Yeah, Rhydian's a real live wolf,' Liam yelled before launching into a mock-wolf howl of his own. Jimi and Sam could not resist joining in, which only made the Ks laugh even louder.

Bernie had seen and heard enough. 'Are you going to take him out, or shall I?' he said gruffly to Rhydian.

Rhydian glared furiously at Liam and the others. 'I'll do it!' He bundled his distraught young brother through the door as the mocking howls and laughter continued. Bryn was trembling with fury and close to tears.

'Bryn, Bryn, it's all right,' Rhydian said. 'They didn't mean any harm.'

Bryn turned on him viciously. 'No! You're right; you are one of them! Go laugh with your human friends, that's where you belong now!'

He pulled away and ran towards the woods. Rhydian was on the verge of following but he stopped. There was something he needed to say to the jokers in Bernie's.

The laughter died away as they saw Rhydian's stony face. 'You think you're funny?' he said coldly. 'Laughing at a confused kid? You see someone different and treat him like he's a joke. We'll, you're the joke, all of you, because deep down you're scared of anyone who isn't exactly like you!'

No one said a word; not even Jimi came back with one of his familiar sarcastic quips. There was only silence and guilty looks as Rhydian shook his head and walked out.

Behind the counter, Bernie sighed. 'Things were a lot quieter before that lad moved here.'

Twenty-eight

There was only one way out of the house for Maddy and she had to take it. The windows all had deadlocks, the doors were secured with their keys removed; the only possible exit point was through her dad's workshop. And he was working in there; the intermittent sound of his electric wood sander made that obvious.

Maddy crept down the stairs, hoping to avoid her mother. She peered into the kitchen. She could sense her mother, but her scent came from another part of the house. Maddy had to move quickly.

She opened the door to the workshop. Her dad, wearing a mask over his mouth and goggles to protect his eyes, was hunched over the bench, using the sander to smooth a length of wood. Soundlessly, Maddy lifted another of the filter masks from a hook and then moved to the garden door. The latch made the tiniest of clicks as it raised but the drone of the sander covered the sound. Slipping outside, Maddy closed the door and tiptoed across the garden. Then she began to run, at Wolfblood speed, for the woods, hoping desperately that Shannon and Tom were still waiting at Bernie's.

But it was a forlorn hope. Shannon, with Tom at her heels, had grown tired of waiting for her other friends, and had stormed out much earlier, long before Bryn and Rhydian made their dramatic appearance.

Shannon was on a mission to save her wolves and was getting on with it, with or without Maddy and Rhydian. She had returned with Tom to the site of the showdown with Kyle and they were working their way through the trees and bushes, searching for the canister of wolf bait.

'I'm not exactly sure where I threw it, Shan,' Tom called. 'And it was dark, remember; things look different in the dark.'

'Just keep searching, Tom.'

They worked their way across one area and then moved to another. And then Shannon gave a squeal of joy as she spotted the metal canister resting against the base of a tree. 'I've found it!'

Tom came hurrying over. 'Is it damaged?'

Shannon turned the canister over in her hand, inspecting it closely for dents or splits, but it looked completely undamaged. 'It's fine. And Kyle only used it once, there must be plenty left.'

Her finger settled on the spray button.

'Are you going to use it?' Tom said, slightly anxiously. 'Now?'

'We're here to see the wolves, Tom.'

Shannon pressed the button, and kept it pressed as she turned in a slow circle and hazy vapour drifted away in every direction.

Rhydian had caught up with his brother, deciding to risk venturing into the woods. Bryn was sitting against a tree, his head in his hands. He looked up as Rhydian approached and the tracks of tears were clearly visible on his grimy cheeks. 'What do you want, human?'

'To see if you're OK.'

'Why should you care?'

'Look, Bryn, I might not be what you and Ceri want, but I'm still your brother.'

'My *human* brother!'

'Humans aren't evil, Bryn. They may not understand us but that doesn't make them our enemy and there's . . .'

He stopped. Bryn had clambered to his feet. His head was back and he was sniffing the air. 'It's Mum,' he breathed. 'She's coming for us.'

Rhydian nodded, aware of his mother's presence but scenting something more too. The bait. He needed more than his Wolfblood senses now; he needed Eolas. He had to forget the human ways; he had to become as one with the earth and sky, as his mother had taught him.

And then he could see her, tearing through the woods at high speed. Images flashed into his vision, he could see everything: Maddy was running, too, and then Shannon turning in a circle and spraying clouds of vapour into the air with Tom standing nearby.

'Stay here!' Rhydian yelled to Bryn.

Ceri had picked up the scent. It was beautiful, enticing, irresistible. She was racing towards it.

Maddy, racing from the opposite direction, had also picked up the mesmerising scent. She stopped, quickly pulled the mask over her nose and mouth and ran on.

'They'll come soon,' Shannon said to Tom, as she continued to spray. 'I know they'll come soon.'

'Don't you think you've sprayed enough of that stuff now?' Tom asked.

'Might as well use it up,' Shannon said happily.

They didn't see Ceri as she transformed from human to wolf form, but Maddy saw her. They heard Maddy shouting as she ran frantically towards them, ripping off the mask to shout, 'Throw it away! Throw it away!'

They heard the growling behind them and turned to see the slavering, wild-eyed wolf powering towards them. Then they realised what Maddy meant. As Shannon hurled the canister and Tom pushed her to the ground, the wolf leapt high into the air.

For an instant they saw nothing; only heard the whoosh of air and the collision of two heavy bodies, and as they desperately scrambled away they saw not one, but two wolves. They were snarling at each other, circling, snapping, darting forward and retreating back. Ready to fight, ready to kill.

Tom and Shannon edged back, gripped with fear, hardly believing what they were seeing. It was Maddy; it could only be Maddy. Despite her terror Shannon pulled her camera from her coat and began snapping off shots.

And then Rhydian was there. For a second he watched the two wolves and then, in full view of Tom and Shannon, he did the only thing possible and transformed into wolf form.

'Are we going mad?' Tom whispered to Shannon.

'No, Tom, we're not going mad. And we never were.'

Wolf-Rhydian joined the two she-wolves, pushing between them, barging them back, turning his head from one to the other, snarling and snapping, as though barking out orders. There were a few final snarls and growls and then all three wolves fell silent and cautiously backed away. As quickly as they had transformed into wolves they regained their human form. Ceri, Maddy and Rhydian were miraculously back.

A stunned silence had fallen on the clearing but it was broken as Bryn came racing over to his mother. 'Mum!'

Breathing heavily, Maddy turned to her friends. 'It's . . . it's the chemicals. They . . . they make people see things. They . . . they . . .'

'Give it up, Maddy,' Rhydian said softly, 'they know.' He looked at Tom and Shannon and spoke without shame or embarrassment. 'This is my mum, Ceri, and my brother, Bryn. We're all Wolfbloods.'

'Like Maddy,' Shannon said.

Maddy said nothing, but simply nodded.

The sound of an engine punctured the tense atmosphere. The Land Rover lumbered into the clearing and skidded to a halt on the muddy track. Emma and Daniel leapt out.

'What's happened?' Emma called, running to Maddy.

'Your secret's out,' Ceri hissed.

Daniel turned furiously to Rhydian. 'You did this! We invited you into our pack and you've destroyed everything!'

Ceri bared her teeth, ready to defend her son, while Emma snarled and moved up to Daniel.

'Stop it!' Maddy screamed. 'Stop it!'

Emma's eyes turned on Rhydian. 'You need to leave our territory!'

'Mam, no!'

'It's all right, Maddy,' Rhydian said gently. 'She's right, I don't belong here.' He smiled at Ceri and Bryn. 'I have a pack of my own.'

Tom and Shannon had watched it all. Staring in amazement, terrified and fascinated at the same time, they knew without doubt that this was a world in which they had no place. Tom reached across and lightly touched Shannon's hand and when their eyes met he signalled that they should leave. They began to back away.

Maddy saw the movement. 'Shan, I wanted to tell you . . .'

But Shannon had already turned and was running up the track.

'Tom, if you give me a chance, I can . . .'

But Tom shook his head and turned to run too.

'That's it,' Emma said decisively. 'We're going. Get in, Maddy! Now!'

With a last despairing glance at Rhydian, Maddy crossed to the Land Rover and climbed inside. The engine coughed into life and the vehicle pulled away.

Maddy looked back through the rear window and saw that Rhydian was watching her go.

Twenty-nine

This time there were no shadowy or blurred images in the photos. This time there was no mistaking the reality, there could be absolutely no doubt. Here were wolves and here were humans becoming wolves.

Tom and Shannon stared at the images on the computer screen of Ceri and Rhydian and Maddy. Maddy, their best friend; how could she possibly have kept the secret? But she had. All the pieces had fallen into place; everything made sense now.

'She lied to us for so long, Tom,' Shannon whispered.

Tom nodded. 'But what do we do?'

'Stupid Shannon and her stupid stories. Well, this time, I have a real exclusive. No one will ever doubt me again.'

It was still early in the evening. Once they felt certain they were not being pursued they had somehow calmed themselves and returned to Shannon's house to study the photographs. They loaded the images quickly, anxious to be certain that their experience had not been some fantastic dream.

It was no dream; each picture told the story in vivid detail.

Shannon was staring at an image of the wolf fight and preparing to upload it to her website. 'This is it, Tom,' she breathed. 'This will rock the world.'

There was a sudden sound at the open window and Shannon and Tom turned to see Rhydian perched on the sill. He could only have leapt there from the apple tree in the garden. 'You can't do that to Maddy,' he said softly.

Shannon and Tom instinctively drew back; this was no longer just Rhydian, this was Wolfblood Rhydian. They'd seen his power, his strength, his fury.

But he smiled, just like the old Rhydian had sometimes smiled. 'You think you know what it's like to be different, Shannon, to be the outsider, but you have no idea. We're scared all the time, living on the run, afraid of being captured and caged when all we want is to be normal. Like you two.'

Shannon and Tom stared for long seconds, uncertain of what to say.

'How is Maddy?' Tom said at last.

'I don't know. I'm leaving with my family, she's probably leaving with hers.'

'Because of us?'

'You know the truth. Soon all sorts of people will know what you know and a lot of them will be worse than Kyle.' He smiled again. 'And thanks for saving us from him.'

'So it was you two?' Shannon said.

'You did the right thing then,' Rhydian said. 'Do the right thing now.'

Rhydian's framed drawing of the two wolves was on the bedroom wall. Shannon turned to look at it and Tom looked too. 'It's a good likeness,' Shannon said.

There was another slight sound and when they turned back Rhydian had gone.

Daniel was standing in the kitchen when Emma came in with another cardboard box packed and ready to load into the Land Rover. 'I'm just taking essentials and valuables. We can start again when we reach Devon.'

Her husband nodded. 'Three hundred years our family's been in this house. Three hundred years.'

'I know,' Emma answered, fighting back tears.

'Where's Maddy?'

'In her room, trying to decide what to take. I'll go up.'

Maddy was sitting on the floor in her bedroom, surrounded by memories; little mementos of special moments she'd shared with her friends and photographs hastily pulled from bulky frames. So many photographs: Shannon and Tom together, alone, with

Maddy, all three of them together, smiling, laughing, happy. And just a few, too few, of Rhydian: with Tom after the football match, one with Maddy, but mostly alone. Rhydian the lone wolf. She would never see him again; she would never see any of them again.

She glanced up and saw her mum, who came into the room and sat with her on the floor. 'It will be all right in the end. You'll have a new life and you will be happy again. I promise.'

Maddy nodded sadly and put her arms around her mum. They were still hugging when Daniel appeared in the doorway. 'I'm afraid we need to get a move on,' he said gently.

Before they could move there was a tap on the front door.

'Stay here,' Daniel said.

Maddy and Emma got to their feet as Daniel went quietly down the stairs to the front door. He waited, breathing hard, afraid but prepared to fight to the end for his family.

Slowly he opened the door. Tom and Shannon stood there.

'Er . . . hi, Mr Smith,' Tom said nervously.

Daniel nodded, silent. Tom nudged Shannon, who reached into her pocket and took out a camera memory card. She offered it to Daniel. 'I think you should have this.'

'Come in,' Daniel whispered.

He led them through to the living room. Maddy and Emma were already there.

'Shannon's brought something for us,' Daniel said, giving the memory card to Maddy.

'It's all the photographs I took.'

Maddy's eyes widened. 'All of them?'

'And nothing's going on my blog. I'm closing the site down.'

'But why?'

Tom spoke for them both. 'Because you're our friend, Mads, and that's supposed to mean something.'

Emma gestured to Daniel. 'We'll leave you to it for a bit.'

'Yeah,' Daniel said. 'We'll be in the kitchen if you want anything.'

They hurried away and the three friends stood in silence, unsure of what to say next.

'Rhydian told us you were leaving,' Tom said eventually.

'Have you seen him?'

'He came to mine,' Shannon said. 'He . . . explained things. You should have trusted us, Maddy. I wouldn't have told anyone.'

'I'm sorry,' Maddy said.

'You could have told us the truth at any time, Mads,' Tom said, 'but you didn't.'

'I know. You're my best friends and I should have trusted you.'

'So trust us now. You don't have to go. We won't say a word, to anyone.'

Shannon smiled. 'And who'd believe us, anyway?'

Relief flooded through Maddy's entire body. 'Thank you,' she breathed. 'Thank you. And . . . and Rhydian?'

They didn't need to reply, she could tell by the looks on their faces. 'He's gone,' Maddy whispered.

She went to the window and stared out at the darkening sky.

'He loved you, Maddy,' Tom said.

'Did he . . . did he tell you that?'

Tom smiled. 'He didn't need to.'

Ceri was leading the way across the moor with Bryn at her side. Rhydian followed as they walked in silence. They had far to travel that night.

A crescent moon lit their way as Rhydian stopped for moment. So many thoughts were rushing through his mind, so many memories that would sustain him through the dark times and live with him forever. Now the wilderness and an uncertain future beckoned. But it had to be. It was the only way.

He turned to look back for a final time. To the past. And Maddy.

Don't miss

Call of
the Wild

Out now

Read on for a sneak peek . . .

One

Snow lay thick on the ground as a lone wolf crested the frozen hilltop, running at full speed, desperately trying to stay clear of three howling, snarling pursuers.

The chase across the bleak moorland had been long and gruelling, and as the winter sun slipped down the sky and night approached, the three bigger and stronger wolves relentlessly closed on their younger target.

Close to exhaustion, the young wolf paused momentarily in the shadow of a tall tree to glance back towards his hunters, glimpsing their yellow eyes blazing through the misty gloom. There was no time to rest; this was life or death.

Stoneybridge Moor was gradually giving way to the beginnings of dense woodland, so the young wolf turned and plunged onward into the trees.

Much deeper in the woodland nestled the centuries-old home of Maddy Smith and her parents, Emma and Daniel. The house was snug and comfortable, especially in winter, but tonight there were no thoughts of an evening snuggled comfortably in the sitting room. They had completed the preparations for the coming night of the full moon and were making their way down ancient stone steps into the den. The den was comfortable too, in its own way – if you happened to be a wolf. It was more of an animal's lair than a room and had been cut into the solid rock beneath the house. There were rock shelves to lie on, a mud floor and thick branches to claw.

The Smiths were Wolfbloods, and the silvery light of the full moon would see them transform from human form into wolves. Every instinct would then urge them to run wild, explore, hunt and roam freely across the moor and through the woodland.

But running wild as wolves meant danger and the threat of discovery, so every full moon, Daniel Smith led his family down into the den where they remained in safety until daylight, when they returned to their human form.

They were in high spirits, though, and as playful as wolf cubs as they entered the den. In the everyday human world they were constantly aware that transformation had to be avoided, but on the night of the full moon it was inevitable. So despite the frustration of being locked in the cellar, the thrill of taking wolf form meant they were buzzing with energy and excitement.

Daniel locked the door and as he turned to continue chatting his head came into sharp contact with something wooden and heavy. 'Ow!'

Maddy and her mum couldn't stop themselves from laughing.

Daniel rubbed his head and glared at a large wooden owl hanging from the ceiling. 'Who put that thing there?'

'It's a present from Shannon,' Maddy said, stifling her laughter. 'Apparently it's the wise old owl of the forest, keeping a watchful eye on all Wolfbloods.'

The owl did appear to be watching them through huge, black glass eyes.

'It's horrible,' Daniel said, returning the owl's frozen stare.

'Shannon just wants to be part of things, Dad,' Maddy said. 'Tom does, too. They want to help if they can.'

Shannon Kelly and Tom Okanawe were Maddy's best friends, and the only humans who shared the Smith family's Wolfblood secret.

'Mmm,' Daniel answered thoughtfully. 'Well, I don't like the thing, and I don't like the way he's watching us.'

Daniel had no idea that his words were absolutely true – the owl was watching them, and so was Shannon.

Before giving Maddy her gift Shannon had carefully fitted a small movie camera behind one of the owl's eyes and linked it, wirelessly, to her laptop. It was now providing a wide-angle view of the den and Shannon could barely contain her excitement as she watched and waited for Maddy and her parents to transform.

She had made a camp in the woods close to the house and was huddled into a sleeping bag as she stared at the laptop, which was perched on a fallen tree.

Down from the heights of the moor the winter snow had melted away, although as night closed in the temperature was plummeting. But Shannon was so engrossed in watching the screen she hardly felt the cold, and she failed to hear the rustling in the nearby bushes.

'So there you are!'

Shannon spun around. 'Tom!' she said. 'You shouldn't creep up on people. How did you find me?'

'Your mum said you were staying over at Maddy's. So with it being full moon, I knew you couldn't be in the den with them, so I thought . . .' Tom paused as he noticed the moving images on Shannon's laptop. He stepped closer. 'Shannon, you haven't . . . you didn't . . .?'

'It's for *science*, Tom,' Shannon said hurriedly. 'It's vital that we learn all we can about Wolfbloods.'

'Maddy's not an experiment, Shan! She's our friend.'

Before discovering the truth about Maddy and her

family three months earlier, Shannon had been convinced that some sort of wild beast was roaming the moor, and had made it her mission to track it down. Now she was putting the same energy into learning all she could about Wolfbloods, even if it meant keeping some of her activities secret from Maddy.

'It's for science, Tom,' she repeated. She glanced at the laptop screen and her eyes widened. 'And look; look what's happening.'

Tom hesitated, knowing it was wrong to spy on Maddy and her parents, but almost as fascinated as Shannon to learn the mysteries of the Wolfblood den.

'They're transforming,' Shannon whispered.

Tom edged closer and saw for himself the way that Maddy and her parents dropped to all fours and swiftly changed from human form into wolves. But he immediately felt guilty for watching. 'You've got what you wanted, Shan, you've seen it happen. Now, let's go.'

'No, not yet, this is too important to miss. Just a little longer.'

They stared in awe, watching the wolves pad around the den, but then the smallest of the three became agitated, repeatedly jumping up at the old coal chute.

'It's Maddy,' Tom said. 'There's something wrong.'

'Yeah. Why is she behaving like that?'

'Maybe she wants to get out. Maybe she can smell us out here.'

'No, not from in there,' Shannon said, so fascinated by the behaviour of the three wolves that again she was oblivious to the sound of movement in the nearby bushes.

But Tom heard it. He turned to look. 'Shan . . .'

Completely absorbed in her task now, Shannon started using the voice recorder on her mobile to detail what she was seeing. 'Maddy is attempting to get out of the cellar,' she said into the microphone.

'Shan . . .' Tom said again.

'Her parents seem agitated, too.'

'Shannon!' Tom said more loudly, and certain now that someone or something was approaching.

'Of course, this could be their natural reaction to being locked up.'

'*Shannon!*' Tom hissed.

'What?'

A low growl cut through the cold night air, and as Tom and Shannon stared a wolf emerged from the bushes. For a few seconds they were frozen with fear, but then they saw that the wolf looked completely exhausted and was in no condition to attack. It was panting heavily and could hardly lift its head to stare at them through baleful, yellow eyes.

'What do we do?' Tom whispered.

Shannon shook her head. Her eyes were fixed on the wolf. 'Rhydian?'

The wolf raised its head a little higher and stared at Shannon as if responding to the name.

'It is him!' Shannon said. 'It's Rhydian!'

Before Tom could answer a terrifying howl pierced the silence and was instantly answered by a second howl, and then a third.

'And he's brought friends,' Tom managed to gasp.

'They're not friends,' Shannon said. 'Run!'

Wolf-Rhydian somehow summoned the strength to run and Shannon and Tom sprinted after him, hurtling towards Maddy's house.

They reached the back garden, where wolf-Rhydian began scratching frantically at the shutters to the coal chute leading down to the den. But the shutters were held in place by a long metal pole pushed through the two handles. No wolf could move the pole – but Shannon could.

'I'll do it,' she screamed, as the howls of the chasing wolves grew louder and more terrifying.

She grabbed the pole and slid it free, and then Tom yanked open one of the shutters.

'Go!' he yelled to wolf-Rhydian. 'Go!'

Wolf-Rhydian leapt into the darkness and in the same moment, three ferocious, snarling and snapping wolves burst into the yard. They came to a halt as they saw Shannon and Tom standing by the hatch, but then began edging forward, yellow eyes glinting hungrily, vicious snarls emerging from deep in their throats.

Tom, still holding open one of the shutters, exchanged a look with Shannon. They both knew there was only one way to go. Shannon jumped into the coal chute and Tom immediately followed, the shutter slamming down as he plunged into darkness. He landed with a thud as the wolves outside howled their rage.

And then, much closer, Tom heard another deep, throaty growl.

Piccadilly
PRESS

Thank you for choosing a Piccadilly Press book.

If you would like to know more about our authors, our books or if you'd just like to know what we're up to, you can find us online.

www.piccadillypress.co.uk

You can also find us on:

We hope to see you soon!